WELCOME TO T-CITY

Suddenly one of the prostrate shapes on the paveline got to its knees, stood up with great difficulty, and made a couple of faltering steps towards the sidewalk before it overbalanced. The figure had overbalanced because it wasn't used to being without arms.

Phillippa screamed.

Nick Levantine opened his mouth to say something, and he was still trying to tell Phillippa what he thought about her when, locked together, they were swallowed by the much bigger mouth of the vacuum pump.

. . . . With a fullthroated cough the vacuum pump gobbed a half-digested stew onto the paveline, and the moving paveline promptly washed it back. . . . The paveline continued to play the part of determined nurse, while the vacuum pump bubbled and dribbled like an overfed baby . . .

INTERFACE

by
Mark Adlard

ace books
A Division of Charter Communications Inc.
A GROSSET & DUNLAP COMPANY
1120 Avenue of the Americas
New York, New York 10036

INTERFACE

Copyright ©, 1971, by Mark Adlard

An ACE Book

First Ace Printing: August 1977

Cover art by *Paul Alexander*

Printed in U.S.A.

JAN CASPOL CLOSED his eyes, and waited.

The sand beneath his naked body was soft, dry, and warm with the memory of a tropic sun. He flung out an arm, and his idle fingers found here and there a fragile shell and pebbles as smooth as jade. When he turned on his side the sand grains dispersed to accommodate his bare shoulder and delved to receive his hip.

The sand supported him as softly as a bed of velvet cushions. He kept his eyes closed.

For the first time he became aware of a faint sound, a murmurous whisper which rose and fell in the distance like the rhythmic breath of an untroubled sleeper. This regular sighing caressed his ears as tenderly as a hand stroking a frowning brow. He directed his attention more fully towards it and identified the sound of the long Pacific waves, kissing and sucking at the coral reef which contoured the shore, before they sobbed with exhaustion on the golden sands.

From the sea a delicate breeze was blowing, gently ruffling the heat of the departed sun, and expiring among the leaning palms and tree ferns where the leaves stroked each other with a noise beyond hearing. And the breeze carried with it a salt scent from the sea, and an aroma of damp sand, to mingle with the island perfumes of sandalwood and flowers.

Jan Caspol turned on his back again, and opened his eyes.

The sky was almost as crowded with stars as the ground was with grains of sand. His dazzled eyes tracked and back-tracked across the glittering expanse, as lost as strangers traversing well-lit but unfamiliar streets. Then, like a returned exile who suddenly recognizes a homely sign, he saw the Little Bear swinging round Polaris by his tail, and Callisto pointing with her jewelled arm.

So Jan Caspol stretched luxuriously on the warm sand, and listened to the mumbling of the waves, and inhaled the mixed scents of the night air, and looked north at the circumpolar stars to remind himself that he was still on earth and not in paradise.

While he waited, he told himself that he should be as happy as it was possible to be.

A new sound disturbed the air, an almost imperceptible swishing. He turned his head, and discovered that the girl had crawled to his side.

She supported herself on a slender arm and looked down at him. Her hair brushed her brown shoulders, and it was blacker than the palm fronds against the spangled sky. By some magic her eyes were both darker than the night and brighter than the stars.

The girl was naked, apart from the freshly picked flowers in her hair, a necklace of sharks' teeth, and bracelets of shells and coloured seeds on her wrists and ankles. Below the necklace her coffee coloured breasts, with their purple areolae, hung like exotic fruit.

Jan Caspol saw her lips open, and her teeth flash, as her mouth curved deliciously round the words of a song.

> you want
> I give
> pineapple
> I want
> I want
> banana
> I want

His eyes left her mouth, crossed the glinting ornaments of her necklace, and forded the deep shadow between her lifted breasts. Her navel was a black moon crater, and there was a sandy whorl of silver grains around it like stars in a spiral nebula.

> I have
> pineapple
> you give
> banana
> I want
> banana
> banana

Jan Caspol reached out and ran his fingers round the rim of the crater. Her flesh was soft and cool. It dimpled to his touch, and the grains of sand fell away like dry bread crumbs. Her hips were as wide as an embrace.

> you have
> banana
> you want

> pineapple
> pineapple
> I want
> banana
> I give

The song stopped abruptly. Scrabbling with her hand on the ground behind her, she searched until she'd found a suitable pebble. She turned the pebble in her small, brown fingers, until she discovered the sharpest edge.

Jan Caspol watched as she drew the pebble in a short diagonal above the swelling of her left breast, and crossed it with a similar line. The sharp edge of the pebble abraded the skin slightly, and the starlight illuminated the white tracks left on her dark flesh. She looked up, and her smile gleamed.

'What does that sign mean?' breathed the soft voice.

He returned her smile. 'Multiply?'

She laughed, and moved closer to him. He felt the duplicated pressure of her yielding breasts against his side.

Jan bent his head, and his nostrils drank in the honeysweet smells of her body as he tasted the first kiss. Then the whispering of the sea was drowned by the roaring of blood in his ears, the waves of a ravenous longing crashed over him, and the flying spray extinguished the stars.

2

It was the dull booming of the North Sea which awakened Steinberg.

He stared with unfocussed eyes at the convoluted patterns on the ceiling. The sea was rough. It usually was. He imagined the sullen, grey waves trundling heavily towards the sea wall, hurling themselves against it in fury, and then recoiling, shattered and broken, leaving a lattice of undulating white spume as testimony to their frustrated energy.

As consciousness forced its way along the neural paths of the brain, like air into the lungs of a half-drowned man, or blood into a frozen limb, the pain of a remembered dream made him groan. He'd been dreaming about Paul.

Steinberg groaned again, and levered his heavy bulk to the side of the bed. The bedroom light went on when his small feet touched the floor.

Pulling on a dressing gown he made sure there were cigars in the pocket, and stepped into a pair of slippers. He padded across the floor, and the bedroom light went out as the door closed behind him. Lights in front of him switched on in series, and the lights behind snapped off, charting his ponderous course as he plodded along the passageways. The door to the systems lounge slid open at his approach.

'Webern,' commanded Steinberg as he crossed the threshold.

The tape started to run obediently. To the music of Variations for piano, op. 27, Steinberg subsided into a capacious chair which had been contoured to give uniform support to his massive shape. He felt in the pocket of his dressing gown, and selected a cigar. Palpating the cigar between his fingers, he scrutinized the wrapper leaf, smelt it, cut it, and applied a gas flame.

In so far as he was capable of being moved by anything, Steinberg was moved by the music of Webern, and he lay in the chair with his head thrown back.

He liked the serial organization and the interest in counterpoint at the expense of harmony. He respected the quiet, epigrammatic style, and the avoidance of overt excitement. He esteemed the precision and the controlled discipline. Above all, he admired the symmetry.

With his senses registering the pungent tobacco as no more than a faint aroma, there should have been nothing to distract his attention from the music. Webern could usually absorb his attention completely. He regarded Webern as not only the last great composer of the period before the Pre-Denaissance, but as the very distillation of the spirit of music itself.

As the First Movement of the Variations for piano ended, Steinberg remembered his cigar, and removed it to stare moodily at the greying ash. He was scarcely tasting the tobacco, and he was aware that the First Movement had given him less satisfaction than it normally did. Replacing the cigar in his mouth, he directed his mind once more to the analysis of the music.

The diagrammatic symmetry of the Second Movement began to crystallize in the vibrating air. The movement was almost entirely a succession of single notes played by each hand alternately. The basic twelve-note row was in the right hand, starting on G sharp, with an inverted row in the left hand, starting on B flat. Then, after switching hands at note ten, both rows—

It was no use. Thoughts of Paul still intruded themselves. Steinberg flicked his cigar into the atomizer where it disappeared with a yellow flash.

'Recycle,' he commanded.

Steinberg reached out towards an inhaler, which was attached to the side of his chair, and as the Variations for piano recommenced he drew the nasal pouch towards his face.

3

THE STARS BEGAN to disappear in front of Jan Caspol's eyes. The tiny pin heads of the sixth magnitude vanished first, and the stellar scale was dimmed until the first magnitude stars faded together like blown sparks. He was watching the death of a universe.

The centrifugal fan stopped rotating and the sea breeze stopped with it. The sound tapes clicked to a halt, and the sea waves ceased their whispering. But the synthetic perfumes of salt, damp sand, sandalwood, and flowers lingered in the still air like the uncertain memories of a dream.

Where the stars had been, a message now unrolled in fluorescent relief.

> *This scenario represented Honolulu long before the construction of Pearl Harbour or the discovery of Waikiki beach by movie moguls. In fact we have shown you this island paradise as it truly was before the third and last voyage of Captain Cook, the Yorkshire explorer, who—*

Jan looked away, and his eyes fell on his packet of felicities. He extracted one and lit it gratefully.

Above the mauve smoke the message continued to unroll.

> . . . *before the white man brought his*
> *microbes, his alcohol, and the mosquito.*
> *In those far off days the natives lived*
> *carefree lives. The fish swam into their*
> *hands, and abundant food was provided*
> *by the bread-fruit tree, the taro root—*

He started to crawl towards the exit, but didn't succeed in escaping the punch line altogether. The speaker unit which had relayed the love song a few hours earlier was reactivated, and the message became audio as well as visual, when the pre-recorded female voice once again dripped its sticky, treacle syllables.

> *Exotic Scenarios Corporation hopes*
> *that you have enjoyed your stay in the*
> *Hawaiian Islands. and that you will come*
> *again, and that you will tell your friends,*
> *Exotic Scenarios Corporation has a wide*
> *range of scenarios to which it is adding all*
> *the time, and if you—*

Jan Caspol crawled out of the aphrodome into the living module, and immediately came across the necklace of sharks' teeth and the bracelets of shells and coloured seeds which had been discarded in a little heap on the floor. He stood up.

A trail of artificial flowers caught his eye, and through the transparent door of a warm air blower he saw the girl, slowly pivoting with her arms raised above her head in the manner of a flamenco dancer.

'Good morning,' he called.

The glazed panel muffled her reply. ''ave a shower if you want. Next cubicle.'

Jan opened the adjacent door, and as soon as he stepped inside the cubicle warm jets of detergent fluid sprayed his body as gently as summer rain. Through the glazing at his side he could still see the girl, turning like a clockwork figurine, but the outline of her perfect figure was now blurred by the west surface of the intervening panel.

While his skin was being lathered into a froth, he examined two unequal, horizontal rows of shower buttons. The top row had five buttons, ranging from *very hot* to *very cold*. He pressed the second one, which said *hot*. The bottom row had twenty-five buttons, in an alphabetical series, ranging from *attar* to *vanilla*. He pressed the penultimate one which said *unscented*.

The misty shape of the girl was no longer visible through the intervening panel. He pressed the button marked *very cold*, and spent a few seconds gasping for breath in the icy shower, before he slid the side panel and stepped into the warm air blower which the girl had vacated.

With each revolution of the turn-table he received a picture of the girl through the front panel of the cubicle. After the first revolution she was standing in the middle of the floor, with her head thrown well back, stretching and yawning. In the harsh lighting of the module her flesh was now the' blotchy, white colour common to the Citizens. At the end of the second revolution he saw that she'd taken off her black wig, and was scratching her bald head with an irritable index finger. As he ended the third revolution she was standing with her hands on her hips watching him rotate.

'What d'you want for bait, 'andsome boy?'

Jan waited until he was facing to the front again. 'No breakfast for me, thanks.'

'Don't be daft,' she protested. 'You must 'ave summat.'

She picked up a tiny fistful of incandescent material, which she stretched and put her legs into. When Jan came out of the warm air blower she was unfolding a table from the wall, and each time she moved her flicker knickers flashed at him like a heliograph. The knickers were supplied only to full graduates of the college.

'My name's Anita,' she said, looking up and smiling.

'Hello, Anita. My name is Jan.'

He pulled on his clothes, and looked at her curved back as she punched an order into the microwave cooker. She conformed exactly to the deeply researched median gestalt.

The Aphrocollege lengthened or shortened noses until they were precisely one quarter the length of the head. Breasts were pumped with silicones until they satisfied the oedipal norm. Hip bones were flanged with sintered cobalt to increase the apparent width of the pelvic girdle.

It was rather curious, reflected Jan, that in the case of noses the college obeyed the canon laid down by Leonardo, but for the more pendulous extremities they adopted the gestalt criteria of Rubens. It was different altogether, of course, once you departed from the median.

'Come and get it,' she said.

Anita unfolded two dining chairs from the wall, and sat down at the narrow table. He sat opposite her.

It revolted his stomach to watch her eat bacon,

dyed the colour of cochineal, and then start nibbling angel biscuits. He forced himself to eat most of an enormous Comice pear, acidulated with tartaric additives, and ripened in the enzyme stimulator.

Anita swept the dirty stahlex plates into a disposal slot, and tapped liquefied caffeine into two cups. Placing her elbows on the table, she squeezed the corners of her eyes with her thumb nails, and deftly caught the dark-tinted lenses. She looked him directly in the face, with eyes as blue and innocent as a child's.

'D'you like me?' she asked.

He reached across the table, and touched her white arm. 'Of course I do, Anita.'

She smiled, reassured. 'I'm always at the Fun Palace. Seat number 249 in row F. It's the sixth row from the back, on the left of the escalator opposite the main entrance. You can always wait if I'm not there.'

'I'll remember,' Jan said, as he got to his feet.

'Don't go without drinking your coffee. You've 'ardly touched it.'

He moved towards the door, and muttered his usual excuses.

'We'll have a real drink next time,' he said.

STEINBERG INHALED DEEPLY, and the music of Webern receded to the fringes of consciousness. He inhaled again, and the music became inaudible. When he inhaled once more, he was immersed in the familiar but always different landscape.

His consciousness was invaded irresistibly by shimmering, concentric waves of colour, which pulsed with an energy emitted from some invisible source. His mind became a platform on which unimaginable shapes, incarnations of inconceivable ideas, propagated with a spontaneity and variety over which he had no control. Colossal perspectives and intergalactic corridors numbed his brain and whirled his senses along endless trajectories through labyrinths which were suspended outside infinity.

Despite its unfathomable complexity and richness, the vision had a form and a purpose which appeared to emanate from somewhere beyond the reach of perception, like meteors from a radiant. Every pulse and every dilation seemed to have a cause, and to be part of an ontological symphony. Somewhere, somehow, every balance had a counter-balance and every theme had a counter-theme. It was the harmony of the spheres.

And Steinberg knew that the sea flowed in his veins, and that he was clothed with the heavens, and crowned with the stars. His intellect melted away from the edges, like floating ice, and his memory emptied. His mind became a mirror, reflecting objects without perceiving them.

He had penetrated the heaven of the Upanishads, of the Bhagavad-Gita, and of Chuang Tzu. He had reached nirvana, and the holy indifference of St François de Sales.

And he had reached these things without the ritual chanting of Sanskrit formulae, Indian mantrams, Mahayana sutras, Hebrew psalms, or Christian prayers. There was no need for him to resort to the spiritual exercises of Sufic mystics, or the fastings and scourgings of medieval saints.

Instead of having to search for paradise, science and technology had bridged the interface, and placed heaven at his finger tips.

In earlier days the hues of his vision had all been in primary colours, and the tones had been light and brilliant, with crystalline reflections of silver, amethyst, and lapis lazuli. As the years passed these hues had become complemented by the secondary colours, which made the picture tremble with an added liveliness and vividness, and the red shattered into cyclamen, coral, cerise, and flame. The colours were shot through with the lights of cascading jewels, of topaz, ruby, and pearls.

And so with the passing of the years, the colours had become richer and more subtle. It had taken Steinberg a long time to realize that there were other, sinister mutations in his paradisaic landscape.

The yellow had changed imperceptibly to lemon and ochre. The lemon had moved into colder depths of green, turquoise, and blue, and would inevitably proceed through ultramarine into violet. The ochre had blazoned into orange, vermilion, and a late flowering of red, before it subsided into crimson. Tints were turning into shades, and the tones were deepening.

He was glad that the discovery of what was really happening didn't strike him in one blow. The truth dawned gradually, and made the ultimate horror easier to bear.

As the years unfolded, this glorious blaze of colour was marching ineluctably from the lightest end of the spectrum to the darkest. The tones of violet had been insignificant and scattered in the early days, but now they were consolidating, and gobbling up the other colours like a storm cloud.

*   *   *

The praeternatural colours faded, and the recycling music became audible. Once again he was an old, old man, listening to Webern's Variations for piano, op. 27, and brooding about his son.

Steinberg knew that he was hastening towards the darkness.

JAN CASPOL OPENED the door, smiled farewell at Anita over his shoulder, and stepped outside into the vestibule where he almost tripped someone who was walking past.

Opening his mouth to apologize for his forgetfulness, Jan was promptly bumped from behind by someone else who cursed him richly in the Tcity accent. Jan hastily took his bearings, and began to walk. At the end of the vestibule he reached a main corridor, and glanced to the left.

It was a sight which had never ceased to fill him with a mild anxiety. Thousands upon thousands of people, with grim, determined faces, appeared to be advancing shoulder to shoulder upon the very spot where he was standing.

Jan hurriedly obeyed the luminous waymarks in the ceiling, and turned right, submitting himself to the oneway traffic flow of the corridor.

The lines formed by the jointures of side walls and ceiling ran ahead of him, slowly converging in accordance with the laws of perspective, until at an immeasurable distance they seemed to run together in an inky blot, like intersecting lines ruled on a page. But he knew that the walls continued to run parallel for many kilometres after that.

Within this narrowing perspective the people were wedged, like corpuscles being pumped along a capillary tube. Jan looked at the thousands upon thousands of hurrying backs, with their hunched shoulders, and thought that the heads looked like a myriad rubber balls on the surface of a running sea.

He glanced backwards. Behind him the lines formed by the angles of the corridor converged once more at the limits of sight, as if the perspective to the front of him was being reflected in a mirror. But it wasn't a true reflection. Behind him were the featureless white discs of thousands upon thousands of faces.

Jan experienced that familiar sense of elation which people often feel when they find themselves part of a multitude which has a common purpose. It was the exhilaration of Xerxes' soldiers when they crammed into the pass at Thermopylae. Perhaps the sensation was shared, for a short time, even by Napoleon's troops when they turned their backs on smoking Moscow.

For Jan Caspol the feeling never endured very long. He soon felt as if he was walking with dead men, or with the legions of the damned.

A cool, gentle breeze of perfumed ozone blew in his face, and fanned the hair across his forehead. It wouldn't have been difficult to believe that this zephyr was a distant exhalation from a dantesque inferno, and that he was gradually descending to the pits of the sixth circle, all sense of circularity lost in an orbit as wide as the arms of a galaxy.

Jan glanced up at the waymarks which glowed in the ceiling. *Levators on right in 100m. Get into line.* He started to jockey towards the right hand wall, but he'd left it very late and he was badly

placed. The onward pressure behind and on all
sides was too insistent, and after fifty metres he
still wasn't in the correct line.

The next waymark came up. *Caution. Levator
station. Keep moving.* He made a final effort to get
across, tripped, almost fell, and was carried past
the turning with his feet off the ground.

A cyborg began to whistle many kilometres
away, and he told himself never to be such a fool
again.

Trampling had overtaken senescence as the
main cause of death amongst the Citizens. Of
course, *Trampling* didn't appear as a specific item
in the official statistics, and the numbers who died
by trampling were included with others under the
general heading of *Disappearance from General
Register of Citizens*. This method of presenting the
statistics could be justified in a way. When anyone
fell over and was trampled to death, he was flat-
tened and kicked to shreds within a few hours, and
any remaining rags and tatters were cleared away
during the Curfew by the scavenger system.

So anyone who was trampled on disappeared,
and was therefore classified correctly in the last
analysis.

Jan continued to edge to the right as he proceeded along the corridor, but directed his course
more carefully. It was a considerable way, and by
the time the next levator waymarks glared down at
him he was walking close to the wall. He had little
difficulty in seizing this second opportunity, and in
fact the crowd would have swept him into the
seething levator station even if he had changed his
mind.

Scanning the departure screen above the long
series of narrow doors, he pushed himself into

position opposite a non-stop delevator to the ground floor. When the door lifted, the pressure of those behind rammed him into the constricted chamber as tightly as a bullet into a muzzle loader.

The door closed, and the delevator promptly dropped like a stone in the void. Jan immediately experienced a sensation of weightlessness, and the accompanying nausea. The air conditioners in the levators weren't very effective, and the smells in that confined space brought cold sweat to his forehead. He gritted his teeth against the vomit rising in his throat.

The delevator stopped as suddenly as if it had hit the ground. The invisible hand which had been trying to rip his stomach upward from its moorings, now squashed it as flat as a halibut, and a momentary force of several gees buckled his legs.

The door lifted and he reeled out into the thru-way, where a smart kick in the shins from a passer-by turned him in the right direction.

6

'I 'OPE YOU 'ad a pleasant evening in the city, sir?'' asked the man in the swallow-tails and striped trousers.

'Night,' corrected Nick Levantine. 'You always say evening, but it's the nights we come through for.'

'As you wish, Mr. Levantine. I 'ope you 'ad a pleasant — er — night, sir?'

'Excellent, Fred. First rate as always.'

'I'm pleased to 'ear it, sir.'

Nick Levantine stretched luxuriously on the chaise lounge, yawned, clasped his hands behind his head, and pushed off each shoe in turn with the toe of the other foot.

'Do you know who I feel like, Fred?'

'I've no idea, sir. You'll 'ave to tell me, sir.'

'Every time I do this', Nick said, wriggling his toes, 'I feel like Madame Récamier displaying her feet for the benefit of the painter David.'

Fred's smile combined ignorance with incredulity. 'Exactly,' he said.

'Do you know what I'm thinking, Fred?'

'No, sir.'

'I reckon this piece of furniture I'm lying on is the only sensible thing in the room. Apart from the bar. All the rest is a lot of angular junk.'

Nick Levantine waved his arm in a gesture of contempt which comprehended the other objects in the room, dismissing in a moment the work of the finest *menuisiers ébénistes* of Louis XVI.

'And yet, sir, I s'ppose some folk might think a few of the bits and pieces, 'ave a sort of what you might call a kind of elegance.'

'Absolutely not,' Nick said. 'Gilded rubbish, all of it. All of it except the couch on which I am lying. And on which, my dear Fred, a Boucher nymph might well have revealed her more intimate charms, for delighted perusal by gentlemen of true taste and distinction.'

Fred coughed behind his hand, and turned away to a console table. The table stood on tall legs, which after the manner of Georges Jacob turned into winged sirens, who appeared to carry the marble top on their golden pinions. He returned bearing a heavy, silver embossed case, which he opened to display a row of fat havana cigars nestling against the cedar wood lining.

'Would you care for a cigar, sir?'

'Fred. Tell me. Are you a robot?'

Fred proffered the case. 'I wondered if you might care for a cigar, sir.'

'Answer the question!' Nick Levantine demanded.

'I'm sorry, Mr. Levantine. I thought you was joking. I thought you was asking what some folk call a rhetorical question, sir. And as you didn't seem to be in much of a 'urry, sir, I thought . . .'

Nick Levantine showed unmistakable signs of exasperation.

'I perform my duties, sir, in accordance with my training, sir. And as you didn't seem to be in much of a—'

'So you are not a robot,' interrupted Nick.

'No, sir.'

'Then stop acting like one, and don't push cigars under my nose at this time in the morning. I'm not Steinberg.'

'I'm sorry, sir.'

Fred closed the silver case noiselessly, and returned it to the marble top of the console table. Nick continued to lie on his back, with his hands clasped behind his head, and stared at the ceiling.

'I'll tell you what you can do, Fred. You can *gizz sum bait*.'

'Certainly, sir.' Fred smiled obediently at the imitation of the Tcity accent. 'What would you like, sir?'

Nick sat on the edge of the chaise longue. 'To show my distaste for this traditional French setting, I'm going to eat a traditional English breakfast in the middle of it. Grilled smoked back bacon, two sunnyside eggs, cup mushrooms . . . '

Fred had begun to punch the instructions before Nick finished speaking, and a few seconds later he was carrying the completed order towards the oval dining table. He slid the flowered and gilt Sèvres plate onto a table mat cut into the shape of an acanthus leaf.

'Funny thing,' Nick said, as he rolled off the chaise longue, and pushed his feet back into his shoes. 'Last night in the city.'

Fred pulled out a chair which had arm supports carved in the form of mermaids, and a back rest containing slender columns, in the style of Sené.

'Yes, sir?'

Nick sat down, and then yanked the chair up to the table. 'I was in the usual sort of place, somewhere in the Second Sector. An aphrodolly called Linda with a—'

'I know the sort of thing, sir.'

'As I was leaving this morning,' Nick continued, cramming his mouth with crisp bacon, 'I noticed a curious thing in the corner, by the door.'

Fred inclined his head respectfully.

Nick swallowed, and reached for a piece of warm, brown bread. 'It was made out of very narrow stahlex strip, and it had been twisted into something resembling a seated figure. A female figure. It had its head thrown back, and it seemed to be in some kind of trance of ecstasy.'

'You don't mean it was 'and made, sir? What some folk would call a work of art?'

'I certainly do.'

Fred was surprised. 'Queer,' he said. 'Very queer.'

Nick Levantine munched in silence, then pushed his plate away, and drank some hot coffee. He extracted a felicity from a box on the table, and Fred came forward with a light.

'It's remarkable,' Nick said, blowing smoke in the air.

'It certainly is, sir. In this day and age.'

Nick watched the mauve smoke curl upwards to the rococo ceiling, and shrugged his shoulders to indicate that although the matter was remarkable, he was able to dismiss it without further thought. He smoked in silence for a while, mindlessly stroking the breasts of one of the Sené mermaids with his fingers.

'Another cup of coffee, sir?'

'No time, Fred. Some of us still have to work for a living. Had you forgotten?'

Fred inclined his head, and smiled indulgently while Nick pushed the chair back and got to his feet. Nick laughed, threw the end of his felicity into the atomizer, and moved towards the exit door with his right forearm raised.

7

JAN CASPOL PUSHED HIS WAY onto the northbound paveline, and sidetracked into the crowded fast lane.

On right and left the windowless elevations of the beeblocks swept upwards for a hundred storeys, giving to the thruway the appearance of an artificial canyon. Behind their sheet stahlex cladding, hollow-section stahlex spaceframes embraced millions of living modules in the tight symmetry of an endless honeycomb. The layers of cells were as perfectly straight and true as the laser beams of the levelling devices which had been used in their subassembly.

Thruway 1 was the main artery of Tcity's night-life in the southern sectors. The dome of the Fun Palace glided by like a distended bubble. Stylized metallic trees were bolted at regular intervals, parallel to the radial avenues which terminated at its rectangular doors.

Keeping his elbows tucked in, Jan managed to extract a packet of felicities, and put one to his lips. He lit it, inhaled deeply, and blew the smoke above his head. As he looked up through the mauve smoke he saw far above him, between the opposing faces of the beeblocks, a narrow strip of

cloudless blue sky. It appeared to be only a few
centimetres wide, but that was another trick of the
long city perspectives. It was, in fact, as wide as
the thruway.

And it wasn't sky at all, but simply a piece of
blued stahlex. Not that it mattered. The Citizens
had forgotten it wasn't sky, even if they ever knew.

Directly ahead of him, but still a few hundred
metres distant, Jan saw the yawning black cavity
of the vacuum pump. It reminded him of a giant
mouth, and it looked as if it was sucking in the
running paveline like a long strand of chewing
gum. The mouth was muzzled now, as it always
was except during the Curfew, by a portcullis
made from stahlex strip.

Jan sidetracked into the slow lane, and stepped
off onto the sidewalk. Coming out of the subway,
he entered the derelict compound inside the city
walls. He'd left the crowds behind. Nobody came
as far as this on the paveline, and the terminus area
around the vacuum pump was invariably deserted.
The compound was an area of waste land, overgrown with coarse grass and weeds, stinging net-
tles, and meadow barley.

He started to walk across this neglected terrain.
The scavenger system was without effect in this
forgotten corner of Tcity, and his feet scuffed
against pieces of rag and filthy paper at every step.
There was no reason why anyone should ever
come here.

The city wall was very tall, as tall as the beeblocks it encompassed. Jan entered its shadow,
and when he was within two steps of the wall he
casually raised his left arm to flatten his hair.

A door slid open in the smooth metallic surface,

remained open just long enough to admit him, and then closed sharply.

Jan Caspol's feet click-clacked on the polished floor, as if rejoicing in the spacious dimensions of the Gatehouse.

'G'morning, sir.'

Jan smiled. 'Hello, Fred. How are you?'

'Can't grumble, sir,' said Fred, coming forward to meet him. 'And very kind of you to enquire. What can I get for you, Mr Caspol?'

Jan glanced at the gilt bronze clock on the facing wall, and checked it against his chrono, 'Just a coffee, please. I'm afraid I haven't time for anything else.'

'No,' Fred agreed, as he punched the order. 'I 'ear Mr Steinberg can be a bit of a—'

He suddenly realized what he was saying, and stopped. But as he brought the coffee in its delicate porcelain cup, Jan's smile robbed the remark of any indiscretion.

'Thank you, Fred.'

Jan sat in his favourite chair. It was an armchair by Poirié, and its sinuous curves made it a little too early in period for most of the other features in the room.

'It's a pity you wasn't 'ere a bit earlier, sir. You could 'ave 'ad a good breakfast with Mr Levantine.'

Jan gulped at the hot coffee. 'He's been through, I suppose?'

'Just gone, sir.'

'How was he?'

'As 'e usually is. What some folk could call 'is usual ebullient self. Of course, I see much more of 'im than what I do of anybody.'

Jan nodded, as if to accept the implied reproach, and then laughed. 'I don't know whether Nick has a greater capacity for amusement, or whether I have a greater capacity for becoming bored. It amounts to the same thing, anyway.'

'P'raps so, sir.' Fred paused. 'If I may say so, Mr Caspol, it's always a pleasure to 'ave you going through.'

Jan lowered the cup. 'That's a very kind thing to say, Fred. But I don't think you see much of any of us these days, apart from Nick and me.'

'That's right, sir.' Fred coughed discreetly behind his hand. 'I believe Miss Steinberg goes out through the north Gatehouse, and finds her amusement up there, as you might say.'

Jan looked at Fred's expressionless face, and then looked away. Fred wasn't committing himself, but he probably knew something of Val Steinberg's outlandish pleasures. Steinberg had certainly been unfortunate in his children.

'Yes,' said Jan. 'I believe she gets into the northern sectors a little more than she used to.'

He finished his coffee and stood up.

'G'bye, sir. P'raps I'll see a little more of you, sir. A bit of relaxation, you know.'

'Perhaps.'

Jan Caspol walked towards the exit door, gestured, and stepped out into the fresh air of a spring morning. For a few moments he stood with his hands on his hips, breathing deeply. It was stated officially that the air in the city was indistinguishable from that outside, but he couldn't believe that even the most sensitive atmosphere monitors could compensate for this.

He'd never seen more than three autos on the parking ground at any one time, and this morning there was only his own. He slid inside, re-set the co-ordinates on the command screen, and pushed his seat into the semi-reclining position. The auto whispered out of the parking ground, and headed north along the wide coast road.

Jan rolled his head to the right, and looked out at the cold waters of the North Sea. The long waves undulated like steel muscles beneath the dark skin of the water, throbbing with power, until their energy could be contained no longer and they burst their casing in a shower of white sparks.

It seemed to him that this remorseless sea, which was forever pounding at the silver, pulverized sands, and which was forever thrown back, somehow represented the very spirit of this part of England, with its heroic defeat and its dumb poetry.

Because this was a region which had produced no poets, no painters, no musicians, no artists of any kind. Nothing had ever come out of this part of England except iron, steel, and ships from what was now the First Sector, chemicals from the Second Sector, railway engines and bridges from the Third Sector, and coal from the Sixth Sector. Nobody had recorded those brutal days, and now nothing remained.

Except the sea. There was always the black, angry, tormented sea.

And when you looked at the steel muscles of that heavy sea you couldn't help remembering. This was a region which had first won its place on the maps of the world through its skills in the manufacture of iron and steel, and in heavy engineering. The old towns had been born from the copulation of Durham coking coal with siderite ores from the Cleveland Hills, and the first railway

service in the world had played the dual role of
go-between and midwife.

Jan turned his head to the left. Through the
panoramic window he saw a group of red deer,
which raised their heads as the auto passed. The
stags had dropped their antlers, but the new
antlers were starting to grow again inside a cover-
ing of nourishing velvet skin.

Beyond the red deer the southbound monorail
issued from a coniferous forest, which knitted an
impenetrable barrier with its evergreen needles.
But the barrier couldn't conceal everything that
lay behind it. Even the Douglas Firs, which over-
topped the pines and cedars, and strained their
tapered shoulders to add another metre to their
pointed heads, rose to only half the height of the
fractionating tower.

Once you saw the tall tower, reflecting the morning sun, you knew that the sputter mills were hidden by the trees around its southern face. Then on
the northern side, above the trees, you could see
the air shimmering in the heat which radiated from
the vast spheres which held the hot metal.

The auto sang along the coast road. Jan lay back
with his eyes closed, and thought about the old
industries.

The steel industry had died slowly and painfully,
like a giant racked by some creeping disease which
nibbled at the toes and finger tips and then worked
inwards. It had been a process of gradual erosion,
as an ever increasing range of plastics sprouted
from the early seeds of X-ray diffraction. The steel
industry had put up a brave fight, trying to overcome the hopeless diseconomies of reheating, re-
rolling, and rehandling, and losing one market
after another.

The new science of manipulating atomic configurations in order to produce materials for specific purposes swept away the dying remains of the steel industry. The new materials had also made important inroads into the markets for other traditional materials, including the non-ferrous metals, ceramics, concrete, timber, and leather.

Jan opened his eyes, and looked once more at the undefeated sea. When the next and final breakthrough in materials technology came, this coastal strip had achieved a far greater importance than it had ever enjoyed in the days of iron and steel.

The new materials had been made redundant, and the plastics industry had withered like an overgrown weed. Stahlex was as universal, and as essential to modern life, as the air people breathed.

The auto slowed, and turned off the coast road. Decorative stahlex gates, in exact imitation of Styrian wrought iron-work, swung open to receive it.

8

JAN CASPOL WENT STRAIGHT through to his systems lounge.

It was a purposeful room, furnished in a rather austere manner. The pictures had been selected from an antique graphics series, and represented geometric shapes, distorted and rotated in accordance with some primitive punched tape programme. The chairs were made of fine gauge stahlex tubing, and were descended at many removes from the furniture which Marcel Breuer had designed at the Dessau Bauhaus.

He sat in a swivel chair in the centre of the room, and pressed a stud on the console at his elbow. A misted glass of pétillant wine coasted into his waiting hand.

'All right,' he said, and before he sipped the ice-cold drink a voiceprint analyzer had verified his authority, and linked the audio receivers to the sales management support system.

With the glass in his hand, Jan swivelled in his chair to face the wide display screen which occupied most of the opposite wall. 'Any messages?' he asked.

White lettering appeared on the dark background.

yes, from mr tilling of aerospace corp. as follows:–

just a reminder not to miss götterdämmerung with the recorded voice of kirsten flagstad as brünnhilde. it will be transmitted direct from mimed production at bayreuth by satellite at 0315 today. if you continue to prefer verdi to wagner you must be mad. i tried to get you on videa last night without success. so i said schläfst du, caspol, mein sohn?

du schläfst, und horst mich nicht,

& dictated this note

Jan smiled. 'Reply as follows. *Ich höre dich, schlimmer Albe.* Thank you for your reminder. In the interests of understanding prejudice I shall certainly look in.' He paused. 'Anything else?'

The screen blanked, and another message appeared.

yes, mr bendix of north eastern stockholders corp. wants you to contact him. not particularly urgent but wants you to comply as soon as convenient.

He frowned. It was rather unusual for anyone to make such a request without indicating what he wanted to talk about. On the other hand, Jan reflected, Bendix hadn't been Chief Executive at North Eastern Stockholders for very long, and he was probably still finding his way around.

'Remind me about Mr Bendix before I leave the lounge,' he said. 'Anything else?'

no other messages

Jan sipped his wine. 'Let's move on to the news bulletin.'

skf announce they are now making ball
bearings on commercial scale in their space
factory. geometrically perfect spheroids to
nil tolerances are obtained under conditions
of zero gee, &. . . .

Other items of commercial, technical, and political intelligence followed, as the bulletin uprolled at a reading speed of 1,500 words per minute. Jan Caspol's eyes held a middle course in the centre of the screen, and he absorbed each item of news as it passed. The concluding item announced that Queen Elizabeth III was to undergo a pregnancy test.

'Now,' he said, when the daily news bulletin had finished. 'Let's get down to the order book. Any divergences?'

no significant divergences from forecast, do
you want details?

It was always the same. The largest divergence ever recorded was only •170, and sometimes he couldn't help wishing that there would be a wild and spectacular departure from trend. There was never any real need to examine the detailed figures, but from time to time he did so, partly to refresh his memory with the pattern of the business, and partly so that he could answer the unnecessary questions asked by Steinberg.

'Yes,' he said, rather wearily. 'Let's have a look at them.'

The display screen projected a statistical table, which occupied its entire surface. The first column was headed *consumers,* and underneath there was a list of manufacturing customers—Government Departments, big specialist engineers such as Aerospace Corporation and Groundcars Corporation, and a few giant enterprises such as GK.

Moving from left to right across the statistical table, the subsequent columns showed for each customer the historical sales in an annual series, current sales, forecast sales, and divergence expressed in terms of standard deviation from expected trend. The exponentially smoothed forecast figures were derived from segmented mathematical models, of which the parameters were continuously updated by applying batteries of regression techniques to the end-uses of stahlex.

Jan's eyes traversed the data from left to right. 'Fade,' he said.

The display screen blinked, and presented another table. The general layout was the same, but this time the first column was headed *stockholders,* and underneath there was a list of the regional stockholders—West Country Stockholders, Wales Stockholders, South Eastern Stockholders, and so on. These stockholders fulfilled the vital functions of supplying stahlex to customers whose demands were too small to justify direct purchase from the Stahlex Corporation, and they supplied heavy tonnage to the big engineers as well. It was the steady and unvarying flow of orders from the stockholders which enabled the Stahlex Corporation to run its plant at optimum efficiency.

Moving from left to right across this second statistical table, the subsequent columns showed the required statistics in the same manner as before.

'Fade,' he said.

Jan Caspol swallowed some more wine, and reflected that it would be a surprising thing if there were ever a significant divergence from trend.

It was only very, very rarely that an unexpected change in demand was revealed. The reason for this was that comprehensive data collection, together with a host of inter-disciplinary techniques and sophisticated methods of market forecasting, made it possible to anticipate changes in the economy long before such changes actually occurred.

Sampling techniques had been refined to the point where even very small surveys could be made to yield population parameters which were guaranteed to be within the finest limits of accuracy. In fact, however, data collection was so comprehensive that sample surveys had virtually become superfluous.

Statistical returns were mandatory for all sectors of production and distribution, and random but frequent audits resulted in heavy penalties if it was discovered that any information given was not scrupulously accurate. Spontaneous changes in consumer spending were unimportant, but even in that area the General Register of Citizens was expected to reveal any changes in taste.

This universal data collection, and its immediate collation and analysis, gave the government a detailed and up-to-the-minute map of the economy, and all this information was freely available to commercial enterprise. This meant that unexpected changes in demand were located almost before they began, and economic activity could be adjusted accordingly.

Jan pushed his empty glass towards the return chute. Yes, he reflected, the economy was now as transparent as a strip of processed nerve tissue seen through a microscope. The days when the economy could spring surprises were long since over.

He redirected his attention to the job in hand. 'Are there any orders outstanding where the delivery request will not be met?'

no

'Are there any complaints?'

> *yes. groundcars corp. allege intermittent cracking at interface during shell forming. they have put samples aside, & have experienced no recurrence.*

'Shit!' Jan shouted at the audio receivers. 'What are we doing about it?'

> *mr levantine is viewing samples by video, & will issue report.*

'O.K. Give me a buzz if they have any more trouble. Anything else?'

> *no, but you wish to be reminded that mr bendix of north eastern stockholders corp. wants you to contact him as soon as convenient.*

'Yes,' Jan replied. 'But let me have a look at his file first.'

9

A COLOUR PICTURE of Bendix's head appeared, rotating in three dimensions. The white lettered text appeared underneath.

facial characteristics: most prominent feature is eyes, which are exophthalmic, probably due to. . .

'Skip that,' said Jan. 'I know what he looks like.'

The screen flickered and presented another colour picture of Bendix, but full length this time, bending down to open the door of a china cabinet. Bendix extracted the figures of an apostle, which he held upside down and brought to within a few centimetres of his eyes, presumably to examine the potter's mark.

bodily characteristics: height 1•68m. weight 69•8kg. . . .

'All right, all right,' Jan moaned. 'Don't be dumb. I said I knew what he looked like. He's an endomorphic cyclothyme with a tendency to hyperthyroidism. Cut out everything except education, interests, and motivation.'

The screen blurred momentarily as the file raced, but then the white lettering of the narrative reappeared and resumed its upward course.

'And run at double speed,' he added. 'I only want to skim it.'

The text immediately began to uproll at a reading speed of 3,000 words per minute.

education
  intelligence: genetically engineered IQ
  estimated at 180.
  formal studies: standard six-year course in
  management science specializing in dta
  (decision theory analysis) at cambridge
  (trinity college) plus two years research in
  automatic systems technology (harvard) &
  one year in cybernetics (helsinki)
  praxis: first appointment in city
  administration. . .

Jan lit a felicity, without interrupting his vision. His eyes continued to follow a middle course as the narrative scurried upwards over the screen. Bendix was very much the average sort of Executive.

interests
  intellectual: history of northumbria (fanatic).
  meissen porcelain (collector of kändler figs.
  from monkey bands & it. com.). otherwise
  favourite period is fourth qtr of 18C: literature
  french (esp. rétif de la bretonne, laclos,
  beaumarchais, chénier); painting also french
  (esp. fragonard); music german; furniture
  english.

> *sexual: married & apparently happy. wife*
> *exhibits standard heterosexual gestalt criteria*
> *except for flattened mammae. this may reflect*
> *gestalt preference, because when subject was*
> *in tangier. . .*

Jan inhaled, and blew the smoke sideways. Bendix was a very ordinary kind of person.

> *motivation*
> *all usual metanergic drives. in addition, there*
> *is thwarted desire for popularity which*
> *almost amounts to wallenstein complex, & it*
> *may be. . .*

'Fade,' he yawned. 'Get me Mr Bendix.'

He turned his chair towards the video. The screen blinked, and Bendix stared into the systems lounge with his exophthalmic eyes.

Jan Caspol's smile switched on within a microsecond of the video, as if they were both activated by the same circuit. 'Good morning, David. How are you?'

'Hello, Jan,' said Bendix. 'I'm sorry to trouble you.'

'Not a bit. Pleasure to see you, David.'

Bendix leaned forward, and his eyes seemed to stand proud of the screen. 'Now that I'm settling down at North Eastern Stockholders, I thought it might be useful if I had a look round your works. I don't want to be a nuisance to you personally, but I wonder if you could arrange it for me?'

'Of course. Delighted.' Jan's smile broadened, and he exuded geniality. 'I'd have invited you over shortly, in any case, even if you hadn't mentioned it. When would you like to come?'

Bendix appeared to hesitate. 'What about tomorrow? I know you must be very busy, and it doesn't give you much time to—'

'That's fine, David. Tomorrow will be absolutely perfect. How will you come? Auto or thopter?'

'I thought I'd come by auto.'

'Excellent,' Jan said. 'You'll find my co-ordinates in the Executive Directory. Revert to manual when you find yourself inside the gates, and park where you want.'

'Thank you, Jan. What time will you expect me?'

'What about 1200? Needless to say, I'm expect-ing you to have a bite with me.'

'That's very kind. Thank you. And there's one other thing.'

Jan smiled. 'Yes?'

'I said I didn't want to be a nuisance to you personally, and I'm not expecting a personally conducted tour of the works. I assume you have a mystagogue?'

'Of course,' Jan said. 'I'll arrange all that. But I look forward to seeing you *in propria persona*.'

'*Persona grata*, I hope. Thank you once again for your kindness.'

Jan's smile was dazzling. 'It will be my pleasure, David.'

The screen faded, and Jan's smile faded with it. A stream of obscene expletives, which burst from his lips with cathartic effect in half-a-dozen lan-guages, was recorded on the filing tapes and trans-ferred to that part of the data bank which was devoted to transactions with North Eastern Stockholders Corporation.

Jan made a final grimace, lit another felicity, and felt better.

'Mr Steinberg,' he said.

10

STEINBERG'S ENORMOUS HEAD, with its massive brow dwarfing the features beneath, appeared almost too big for the video screen.

'Good morning, sir,' Jan said.

'Anything to report, Caspol?'

Steinberg's words reverberated in the systems lounge. The tone control on his terminal attenuated the higher frequencies, and amplified the lower, thus deepening the tone of his voice to something nearer normality.

'Everything is running smoothly, sir, except for a quality complaint.'

Steinberg screwed his features up like a paper bag, and blew them back to standard size with the forceful expulsion of a monosyllable. 'What!'

'Nothing serious,' said Jan hurriedly. 'Isolated cracking along the interface in the shell department at Groundcars. Mr Levantine is having a look at it and—

'I'll get details from Levantine when I see you all this evening.'

Jan concealed his chagrin. It sounded as if there was going to be another 'get-together'.

'Anything else?'

'Only one other thing worth mentioning, sir. Mr

Bendix, the new Chief Executive at North—'

'Get on with it, Caspol.'

'Sorry, sir. At Mr Bendix's request I've invited him over tomorrow for a tour of the works.'

'Hm. You will entertain him at lunch.'

'Yes, sir.' Jan almost added *naturally* or *of course*, but realized just in time that it would sound impertinent.

'Do you have facilities to suit his personality profile?'

'Yes, sir. I'll use the Georgian room, and—'

'Anything else?'

'No, sir.'

'Be at the Seaton Hotel at 2130 this evening. I'm inviting everyone.'

Jan twisted a smile. 'Oh, thank you—'

But Steinberg had disconnected, and the screen was blank. It was another example of what Nick Levantine referred to as Steinberg's 20th-century manners.

11

NICK LEVANTINE'S AUTO NOSED OFF the coast road and hissed through a wide gateway to the Seaton Hotel.

The circular garden in the middle of the autopark looked gay and colourful, despite the evening dusk. There was a blaze of forsythia, like a swarm of tiny yellow butterflies. Crocuses flared white and purple against clumps of dark green schiaparelli, which had been mutated from the original stock brought back with early scrapings from the crust of Mars.

The auto circumnavigated the garden, homed onto its numbered parking spot, and sighed to a standstill. Nick got out and looked around. The only other autos were the dummies which never left the autopark, and which were switched around the parking spots every night.

Nick ran lightly up the stone steps, and doors at the top swung open to receive him. As he crossed the thick pile carpet in the hall an immaculate figure emerged from a shadowy alcove, with slicked hair, silver-dusted sideboards, a glittering tie pin, and trousers with creases sharp enough to have taken the beard off Barbarossa.

'Good evening, sir. Welcome to the Seaton

Hotel. If you should require anything you cannot find, sir, you have only to ring from the bar.'

Nick paid no attention, and went straight through to the bar where he immediately thumbed his favourite stud. A heavy, traditional glass, multi-faceted and with a moulded handle, was dispensed into his waiting fist. He assessed the contents for a moment, the dark body and the kingly white crown, then crooked his elbow and swallowed mightily.

'Ah-h-h.'

He gave a resounding belch, and wiped the froth from his top lip with the back of his hand. It was the historic drink of Northumbria, and in olden times it had been the solace of those armies of men who laboured in the ancient trades—coal miners, boilermakers, platers, riveters, stevedores, and the gangs who sweated at blast furnaces and steel melting shops, and in forges and rolling mills.

It was the best drink in the solar system, reflected Nick, and probably in the universe. It was worthy to be carried in gold cups by blushing Hebe, and its fairy foam was fit to wet the bearded lips of Zeus himself when he relaxed upon Olympus's top and gazed upon the follies of all mankind.

Nick Levantine drank again. He told himself that it was a major triumph of modern technology that he could still obtain, in all its pristine glory, the original Newcastle Brown Ale.

Placing his glass on the bar he turned to face the room. The low ceiling glowed with a faint luminescence, which shed its light upon the scene below. There was just sufficient activity in the room to provide an illusion of bonhomie without giving the impression of overcrowding. Faint strains of a concerto by Raphael Rozier drifted in the air.

At the stahlex-topped tables the figures sat. By the door one was speaking earnestly, and illustrating a point with eloquent hands. A neighbour listened, head cocked on one side, with every appearance of rapt attention. On the other side of the room an intimate group seemed to be laughing over a risqué story, and they were slapping the sides of their chairs in delight.

Another figure at the nearest table had been staring fixedly at Nick for some time. Now it stood, moved its head right and left to establish focus, and walked up to the bar.

'Good evening, sir. Would you like to talk?'

'No,' said Nick.

'I can talk about the influence of Zoroastrianism on the curried dishes of the Parsees, the Palladian double cube, and how itaconic acid was used to improve the dye receptivity of acrylonitrile copolymers.'

'Go away,' Nick said.

'Thank you, sir.'

The figure returned to its seat, and Nick swung back to face the bar. As he finished his drink there was a discreet tap on his shoulder. He turned to face another figure.

'I can talk about the use of solid-state lasers for investigating transient effects in plasma research—'

'Get to hell out of it,' Nick yelled, his words overriding the rest of the pre-recorded speech.

'Thank you, sir.'

He watched the autopal return to its seat, and the moment it was seated an adjacent figure stood up, and started towards the bar with a determined step. Nick crashed his empty glass on the bar, and pressed a contact button.

'Listen,' he bawled into the speaker. 'Is that Hotel Control?'

'Yes, sir,' came the reply, in two phonemes of equal pitch.

A suave voice spoke over his shoulder. 'I can talk about the astronomical discoveries of the Mayas, Abu Bekr and the caliphate—'

'Levantine speaking,' he said.

'Yes, Mr Levantine,' said the unaccented voice.

'I've a very strong complaint to make.'

'—and the circadian rhythm of fiddler crabs.'

'I've told you before', Nick shouted into the speaker unit, 'that when I come in here I want a quiet drink, and not be pestered half to bloody death by your greasy robots. There's only one chance in ten thousand million that I'd want to listen to anything these ninnies can talk about anyway. And I want to be quiet. *Quiet!* Do you understand?'

'Yes, sir. It's just that you appeared to be alone, and your apparent loneliness switched on their fraternization programmes.'

'Switch them off then,' yelled Nick. 'I'm not lonely. And if one of those ambulating sound tracks accosts me again I'll kick it right in its waveform guide detector.'

He pressed for another Newcastle Brown Ale, and looked round briefly to ensure that there were no further signs of his being bothered.

The autopals were very subdued. They sat huddled together at the stahlex-topped tables, in groups of threes and fours. The air was filled with a gentle twittering, as they played their programmes to each other *sotto voce*.

The door opened, and Nick looked up quickly. He had feared that the next to arrive might be

Phillippa. But it was only Arnold Wilkins, the Comptroller, who looked anxiously into the room.

'Hiya, Wilkie,' he called, somewhat relieved. 'Come and talk to me about naked women or something. It's the only thing these idiots don't know anything about.'

12

WHEN JAN CASPOL ARRIVED at the Seaton Hotel, all the other Executives were already there.

Nick Levantine, the Production Executive, always caught the eye first. Nick was one of those people who seem determined to play the rôle of protagonist in a drama of their own devising. He strode through like like Charles the Bold through the pages of Philip of Comines of Clovis through those of Gregory of Tours, or perhaps even more like the Black Prince through the chronicles of Froissart.

'Here you are, Jan,' said Nick, handing over a pint of Newcastle Brown Ale with proselytizing zeal. 'Splash your pipes with this.'

Phillippa Mercer, the Engineering Executive, smiled at him faintly and returned her gaze to Nick. Her Fra Angelico profile was softly illuminated by the indirect lighting.

Gerry Peters, Public Relations Executive, was pretending to bubble with enthusiasm about a new advertising project which he described with energetic movements of his hands. Arnold Wilkins, the Comptroller, was listening to him with the solicitous expression which was permanently stamped into his anxious features.

All the Executives were there except the Chief
Executive. Steinberg was never early, and he was
never late, and he would never tolerate lateness in
others. Jan looked at his chrono. It was 2125.

It was the first time Jan had actually met his
fellow Executives, except for Nick, since the previous get-together several months before. Even
so, there was very little any of them could find to
say to each other. Gerry Peters frothed and subsided into silence like a boiler which had popped
its rivets.

'Did anybody watch Götterdämmerung?' asked
Arnold Wilkins, in an inspired attempt to oil the
wheels of conversation.

They fell upon the new topic gratefully. Phillippa said she thought the miming of Brünnhilde,
when she chose to die with Siegfried in her arms,
was magnificent.

Gerry Peters waved his half-empty glass, con-
ducting an inaudible Twilight *motiv*, while he
began to deliver the third Norn's prophecy in an
assumed soprano.

> *Es ragt die Burg*
> *von Riesen gebaut;*
> *mit der Götter und Helden*
> *heiliger Sippe*
> *sitzt dort Wotan im Saal.*

The door opened and Steinberg came in.

Wilkins spoke first. 'Good evening, sir. May I
get you a drink?'

Steinberg lumbered towards the bar as if intent
on physical assault, and Wilkins stepped aside.
Steinberg leaned heavily on the contact button.

'Hotel Control,' he gasped. 'Remove the environment supports.'

'Certainly, Mr. Steinb—'

Steinberg lifted his thumb and cut the response. The music of Raphael Rozier stopped dead, and the autopals around the tables got to their feet like one robot. Those nearest the door went out immediately, and the rest formed an orderly queue to await their turn.

Wilkins tried again. 'May I get—'

'Malt,' said Steinberg.

The remaining autopals filtered out of the door, and Steinberg took up a position in the centre of the room. Arnold Wilkins bent over a personal console, and the other Executives grouped themselves round Steinberg like the four Galilean moons of Jupiter. Wilkins collected the drink, and gravitated into the same orbit.

To anyone who'd seen only Steinberg's head on the video, the rest of his body came as a shock. Despite the massive head, and cumbersome physique, Steinberg was a very short man, little more than a dwarf as far as height was concerned.

He lifted the drink in his podgy hand. The whisky had been dispensed into a Queen Ann cordial glass with an air-entrained stem, and his monogram was etched into the cup with cursive script.

'Levantine.'

'Yes, sir.'

'What's this I hear about cracking along the interface at Groundcars?'

The other astonishing thing about actually meeting Steinberg, away from the video network, was his voice. Deprived of the terminal tone control his voice was as thin and high pitched as a toy whistle.

Nick Levantine began by describing the results of his examination, and went on to show how they exemplified the principles of molecular geometry.

Steinberg examined a cigar as he listened. His enormous, depilated head shone with reflected light under the ceiling illumination. The skin was so tightly stretched across the swelling cranium that it looked as if it would split, and the outlines of sutures and trepanning operations were clearly visible. Most Executives wore toupees to hide the evidence of neuronal amplification, but Steinberg displayed his surgical blemishes as proudly as Heidelberg duelling scars.

'You're not trying to tell me, are you, Levantine, that the material really is defective?'

Jan Caspol felt sorry for Nick, because that was precisely what he was trying to say. Nick was forced to admit that there was evidence of a random variation in the control conditions of the Sheet Sputter Mill, which could have accounted for some imperfect meshing at the interface, but this had now been corrected.

'Mercer?'

'Yes, sir.'

Steinberg lit his cigar, while Phillippa explained how the continuous monitoring system had come up with an automatic alarm signal, but that the default routine had been overridden by material flow control. She added that steps had been taken to ensure that if it ever happened again there would be immediate intervention.

'I must conclude', Steinberg said, his voice sinister, 'that there is a risk of similarly defective material having been dispatched.'

'Yes, sir,' replied Phillippa. 'But only a very minute quantity.'

'Have we any means of tracing it?'

'No, sir.'

Steinberg was grim. The deeply incised lines which ran downwards from the corners of his mouth gave his chin the appearance of a component part, engineered to an exact fit, and pressed into place.

'Let's hope it will not be used in a very critical application,' he said, with bitter menace, to both Nick and Phillippa. He turned slightly. 'Caspol.'

'Yes, sir.'

'Are all the arrangements made for Bendix tomorrow?'

'Yes, sir.'

'Who will take him round the works? Henry?'

'Yes, sir.'

Jan Caspol restrained a smile. There was something wildly uncharacteristic about Steinberg using a first name. It was like hearing an Archbishop swear. It almost created a sense of comradeship.

'Wilkins.'

'Yes, sir.'

'I've been having a look at your revised algorithms for heat-sinking. You appear to have forgotten that . . .'

Arnold Wilkins turned his worried face sideways, partly to give the impression of listening intently, but mainly to avoid inhaling Steinberg's garlic-laden breath. His eyes were swivelled askew towards the Chief Executive. Wilkie had straight black eyebrows which joined over the bridge of his nose, and his expression gave the upper part of his face the appearance of two quavers joined by a ligature.

As Comptroller, Arnold Wilkins was responsible for constructing the economic models which simulated and quantified all the corporation's activities, and for setting down optimal methods of operation.

Comptrollers, with their basic disciplines in DSM (Discrete System Math), had taken over the functions long exercised by accountants. After a jealous struggle to retain the favours of the goddess of commerce, the accountants had been cast off with the counters of cowrie shells and buffalo skins, the goat-herds, the silver-smiths and the country bankers, to join the nostalgic roll call of those defunct trades which had used their clumsy yardsticks to measure wealth. Accountants were remembered, when they were remembered at all, as the romantic students of Luca Pacioli, and as the men who kept the books for merchant adventurers to East India and Hudson Bay.

Jan Caspol looked at Steinberg's eyes. The eyes were dim and cloudy, and the irises were an indistinguishable colour beneath their thick contact lenses, like nondescript coins seen through the bottoms of waterfilled jars.

'Peters.'

'Yes, sir.'

'How long before your latest piece of nonsense comes out in public places?'

Gerry Peters tried to appear amused. 'Two days, sir.'

Jan looked once again at those filmy eyes, and wondered what life now meant for Steinberg. Children were supposed to be the consolation of old age, but Steinberg's children must have caused him more sorrow than joy. Val, who had a job outside the Stahlex Corporation as City Executive, was too intent upon her own grotesque pleasures to bother with her father. And Paul . . . What had happened to Paul?

As Jan looked at those filmy eyes he was suddenly moved by a feeling of pity, touched with fear.

Steinberg was standing in the middle of the room like a man who had been dumped down on the shore of an Azoic sea, with primaeval rain hissing on the bare rocks. There were no fish in the sea, nor creatures on the land, nor birds in the air. Even if he spent the rest of his life searching, even if he dug frantically among the stones on the beach and filtered the water from the intertidal pools, looking in desperation for the first feeble life of a zoophyte, the meandering track of a sea-worm, Steinberg would never find anything, anything at all, which moved with a life of its own. Steinberg was as alone as if he had existed before time began.

But now Steinberg unclamped his jaw, and fluted the syllables which freed them from his presence. He propelled his swollen bulk across the floor on inadequate feet, and the door opened at his approach. Wilkins and Peters bobbed out in his wake. Phillippa made as if to follow them, and then wavered.

Nick turned to the bar, and punched out another two pints of Newcastle Brown Ale.

'Would you like another drink, Phillippa?' asked Jan.

She glanced at him gratefully. 'A little more juice, please.'

'What a farce,' Nick said, wiping his mouth on the back of his hand. 'What a stupid waste of time.'

Jan nodded. It was difficult to see any point in the meeting they'd just had, or indeed in any meetings at all.

Direct and instantaneous audio-visual communications had made face-to-face contacts quite unnecessary in the management of any enterprise. There was no real need for any of the Executives to meet each other for purposes of administration. And yet Steinberg insisted on these occasional get-togethers where he asked a few questions, and gave a few directives, all of which could easily have been fed into the cybernet which embraced the various management support systems.

'It's part of his 20th-century manner,' concluded Nick, not for the first time.

Jan reflected that it was curious how Steinberg had become entangled in discredited psychological theories, and how he should feel it necessary to pay lip service to such outmoded managerial concepts as *team spirit* and *participation*.

The autopals began to file back into the room, nodding and grinning like forgiven children, and shuffling with abbreviated steps so as not to trip each other. The music of Raphael Rozier floated on the air.

Nick gulped at his drink. 'One more for the road, and then I'm off.'

'Where?' asked Phillippa.

'Into the city. Where else?'

Phillippa spoke quietly. 'I can't think why you should want to go there every night.'

'My hair grows quickly,' said Nick dismissively, and turned away to the bar.

Phillippa appeared as if she were going to say something else, but decided against it, and walked out.

'I hear there's a new club,' Nick said. 'The Fiesta Club. Off the thruway in the First Sector. I thought we'd see what it was like.'

'I was in the city last night,' Jan replied.

'So what?'

'The pleasures of the city no longer have the same unending fascination for me that they have for you.'

'Come on,' Nick insisted. 'Drink up. I'm getting a bit worried about you, Jan; a night out will do you good.'

13

NICK LEVANTINE'S AUTO SPED through the darkness of the coast road. Exactly 100 metres behind, at exactly the same speed and as if attached to it by invisible harness, Jan Caspol's auto followed, containing Nick and Jan on its reclining seats.

'Honolulu,' Nick mused, folding his hands behind his head. 'Was it well appointed?'

Jan was sardonic. 'Everything except the sound of Ne Nes.'

'Ne Nes?'

'Hawaiian geese.'

Nick rolled his head sideways to face Jan. 'What are you thinking about', he asked, 'apart from the deplorable gaps in my general knowledge?'

'I can't help thinking about Steinberg,' Jan replied. 'What sort of pleasure do you think he gets out of life?'

'He's the boss man at Stahlex, isn't he?'

'Yes,' Jan agreed. 'But a man of his intelligence can't get any satisfaction out of mere power and authority.'

'All right.' Nick sounded bored. 'What about pleasure in a job well done?'

'Insufficient,' said Jan. 'Automatic management support systems make the job child's play.

Except', he added with a chuckle, 'for the occasional quality complaint.'

Nick grunted, and wasn't inclined to pursue the argument. Jan looked out of the window.

The muscled sea glistened like carved ebony, and moon-white foam sparkled on the crests of the black waves. No sound penetrated the auto, and the sea waves crashed in silence, like a vision in a dream. Jan slid a panel in the panoramic screen, and the muffled roar of the straining waters became audible.

'There's something else,' Nick said. 'You're suffering from taedium vitae, or melancholia, or Byronism, or Weltschmerz, or ennui, or Angst, or anomie, or whatever the hell the current vogue word is. What's the matter with you?'

Jan shrugged.

'You must have some idea,' said Nick.

Jan pondered. 'I feel somehow divided against myself.'

'When is your birthday?'

'What?'

'When is your birthday?'

'June nineteen.' Jan was puzzled. 'Why?'

'There you are,' Nick said triumphantly. 'You're a gemini. A typical gemini, even after allowing for precession and the zodiacal shift. Two men in one. Siamese twins without an interface.'

Jan laughed.

'Tell me what you did this afternoon,' asked Nick.

'I watched Götterdämmerung.'

'And then what?'

Jan stretched comfortably in the reclining seat. 'I did what I normally do these days, when the weather is fine. I walked in the garden.'

'And?'

'And watched the birds.'

Nick laughed out loud. 'How pleased Jean Jacques would be, to discover his noble savage in a modern garden.'

'I spent a long time watching a Blue Tit.'

'I'm sorry,' said Nick. 'I've got the wrong model. Not Rousseau, but St Francis. *Noverim me, noverim Te.*"

'It was in the branches of an oak tree. Can you visualize a Blue Tit?'

Nick raised his eyebrows in surprise. 'Now look here, Jan. I mightn't know a Ne Ne when I see one, but I can certainly visualize a Blue Tit. Order *Passeriformes*, family *Paridae*, genus *Parus*, species *Parus caeruleus*. Folk names Tom Tit and Pick-cheese. Length 12•5 centimetres. Prominent field marks are blue cap and white cheeks bordered by—'

'Yes,' interrupted Jan. 'But can you *visualize* it?'

'Of course I can. I can see the colour plate in front of me now.'

'We are all the same,' Jan sighed. 'We know everything, and understand nothing.'

'And what does that transcendental rubbish mean?'

'The bird is never still for a moment,' Jan continued. 'Not for one moment. It vibrates with energy. You see its head pointing one way, and then realize you're wrong, because it's pointing the other way. And before you've registered that fact it's in a different position altogether. Now it's on top of a twig, and while you blink it appears underneath. I felt as if I was seeing a projection from an old cinematograph with a jerky film or a sequence of frames from a time-lapse camera.'

Nick's auto slowed down, and swung into the parking ground. Jan's auto followed, and came to rest on its parking spot.

Jan turned on his reclining seat and looked at Nick. 'Then I had another thought that scared me.'

Nick sat up. 'What was that?'

'I thought that perhaps I wasn't watching a Blue Tit at all. I thought that perhaps I was watching a tiny machine, animated by a microminiature motor.'

Nick Levantine exploded with laughter. 'Be careful,' he said, laughing again. 'Be careful, or you'll find you've turned into a tin St Francis watching tin birds.'

14

'G'EVENING, GENTLEMEN '

Fred was mildly surprised at seeing Jan two evenings in succession, and he wore a special smile as
he brought them two bottles of Newcastle Brown
Ale on a silver salver.

Jan didn't really want another ale, but it was
their last opportunity.

They filled their whisky flasks, and equipped
themselves with money. Fred bowed them towards the door, with hopes that they would have a
pleasant evening.

They crossed the compound, which was deserted as usual. The vacuum pump yawned behind
its muzzle. They mounted the southbound
paveline, and sidetracked into the fast lane.

The dome of the gaudy Fun Palace drifted past.
Nick sidetracked into the slow lane, and stepped
off onto the sidewalk. Jan followed him, and they
crossed to the other side by subway. This was the
edge of the district where most of the aphrodollies
lived. Anita's module was encapsulated somewhere in the beeblock next to the Fun Palace.
Further along the thruway was the Blue Star Club.

Turning off the thruway they entered a narrow street, and when Jan looked up he saw that it was called Vulcan Road. He guessed that they must be near the course of the vanished river, and on the site of the ancient Ironmasters' District.

The name of the road made Jan smile. It was as if the blacksmith of the gods had returned to his ruined domain, to remind men of his forgotten authority. From Vulcan Road tiny alleyways ran left and right, and each one was named after a superseded metal. Jan noticed Silver Street, Zinc Street, Copper Street, Tin Street.

Jan couldn't help remembering that it was on this ground that the world's greatest iron industry had once flourished. Neighbouring streets had once housed a labour force whose skills had introduced the age of steel. The reflected flames of Bessemer converters had turned the black river into a new Phlegethon.

A dark tunnel appeared on their left. Nick led the way into it, and Jan saw that it was called Tubal Lane.

The crowds in the tunnel became more dense, and moved forward with increasing difficulty, as if there was an obstruction in the way. As Jan and Nick edged forward they saw an open doorway, into which many of the people in the crowd were trying to force themselves. A suspended sign said *Anvil Bar*.

'I don't think this is what we want,' Nick said. 'But now we're here we may as well have a look.'

Jan agreed. 'It's easier to go in than to go past.'

They allowed themselves to be carried through the doorway by the swirling mob, and a few minutes later they found themselves in a very large, square room. There were three absolutely blank walls, with plain stahlex benches round them. Naked lights dangled from the ceiling, and the carpetless floor was strewn with empty felicity packets, bits of paper, and a great deal of other rubbish.

Spaced about there were dozens of pedestal tables bolted to the floor, around which people were drinking. Stretching the full length of the fourth wall was an extremely long bar, at which hundreds of men were struggling to reach the beer studs.

The Anvil Bar was obviously one of those Tcity institutions which were devoted to the consumption of the greatest possible volume of liquor in the shortest possible time. The only drink available was high gravity beer, containing a large proportion of hops to wort, as well as the inevitable statutory additives. The beer was dispensed in plain, unbreakable, one litre glasses. The din was terrific.

'No women,' Nick shouted.

Jan looked round the room. He was looking at the descendants of the tough, proud labor force, which had manned the ancient industries. The difference was that their forbears had needed to drink large quantities of beer, in order to replace the sweat lost in melting shops and rolling mills. But these men drank because they'd nothing else to do.

'Come on,' yelled Nick.

Nick elbowed his way across the packed floor towards an exit, and Jan followed. They were finally squeezed out into Tubal Lane like pieces of soap. But it was less crowded now, and they moved ahead more easily.

'There it is,' Nick said, pointing ahead.

The narrow, black wedge of the tunnel stretched

before them, like an entrance to Nibelheim, but above the heads of the shuffling pedestrians there was an illuminated sign. *Fiesta Club*. They pressed on.

Nick pushed at the unpainted door, which swung inwards on squeaking hinges. Jan looked over Nick's shoulder at a steep flight of wooden stairs.

'It's a bit ghostly, isn't it?' laughed Nick.

Jan nodded. 'It looks like a bit of the old town.'

Nick led the way up the stairs. Jan had assumed the stairs were of stahlex, dressed to simulate the appearance of wood, but as they ascended the stairs creaked with the proverbial wooden sound. There was a landing at the top, with a handrail and then an open door.

They entered a small ante-room, so brightly illuminated it hurt their eyes, with a cloakroom to the left. On their right was a rickety table, behind which sat a man in an old-fashioned dinner jacket and neck-tie. The man had dark eyes, a Sicilian moustache, and a dazzling smile.

'Good evening, gentlemen. Tickets here, gentlemen.'

They went over to the table, and Nick put down some coins. Jan observed the precise outline of the moustache, which looked as if it had been painted on, and the perfect symmetry of the teeth, out of which a sharpened stick protruded. Jan concluded that the man behind the pay desk was a dolphin-brained cyborg, or some kind of android, but the creature proved himself to be human after all by miscalculating the change.

'Thank you, gentlemen. Through that door, gentlemen.'

Jan crossed the room, and pulled open a wooden

door. After the brightness of the ante-room everything in the club appeared quite black, except for
some scattered tongues of white light and a dim
glow from one wall.

Jan's eyes accommodated, and he saw that the
floor was laid out with chairs and round-topped
tables, the outlines of which were charcoal-
sketched by the flickering light of candles. At the
other end of the room was a clear space, presumably for dancing, and beyond that a raised platform
on which stood something which looked like an
antique theatre organ. The dim glow in the wall
emanated from a small bar.

'Let's sit down,' Jan said.

They moved over to one of the tables. The table
was covered with a plastic resin, and in the centre
was a lighted candle stuck into the neck of a bottle
labelled Vat 69. The chairs had been mass-
produced out of transparent fibreglass, and they all
appeared to be identical, with unadjustable backs
and arms.

'Well!' Nick said, as he lowered himself gingerly
into one of these primitive artefacts. 'What do you
think of it?'

'A gem. A perfect gem.' Jan looked round the
room. Less than half the tables were occupied. 'I
wonder what happens.'

Nick didn't share his enthusiasm. 'I shouldn't
think anything happens. I'll bet we don't even get a
flicker.'

Jan Caspol reflected that Nick was probably
right.

In addition to the Fun Palace and the Blue Star
there were dozens of smaller clubs, usually fairly
close to the ground, scattered about the side
streets of the First Sector. The exorbitant entrance

charges made them little oases, or deserts rather, amidst the teeming population of the city. The clubs were the only places where a man could drink without literally having his feet trodden on all the time. Such places were, inevitably, ports of call for the aphrodollies, because only barbers and other people with surplus money could afford to visit them.

The Fiesta Club, however, appeared to be in a different category. The entrance charge, for example, had been relatively cheap, and the club was unlikely to be on the flicker circuit.

The air began to tremble under the impact of programmed music. The noise was processed through a battery of modulators and mixers, after which it vibrated the ossicles in Jan Caspol's middle ear, passed through the fluid in his cochlea, and ultimately reached his brain where the sound of an electronic clarinet was extracted and identified.

'It wasn't a good idea,' Nick said. 'I'm sorry I've wasted part of the evening.'

'Not a bit.'

Nick pulled out his whisky flask, and thumbed the valve. 'A quick one for the road,' he said, 'and then we'll return to more civilized parts, starting with the Fun Palace. Are you ready?'

'I think I'll stay.'

'What! You don't mean you *like* it here?'

'It makes a change,' said Jan, 'and in any case, I want to leave before the Curfew. You push on if you like.'

Nick returned the whisky flask, and dropped a hand on Jan's shoulder as he stood up to go. 'I'm getting a bit worried about you, Jan. I really am.'

He left.

Jan stretched his legs under the table. The programmed music had been switched into another sub-routine, and was being automatically recycled with different pitches and tones. He took out his flask, had two mouthfuls of whisky, and decided he didn't want any more.

There wasn't really any point in staying, and he may as well have left with Nick.

As he stood up a red velvet curtain which he hadn't noticed before was swept aside and a girl came out. She walked with long strides to the other end of the room, mounted the raised platform, and sat down behind the antique theatre organ.

The programmed music decayed and died. For a few moments there was silence.

The girl started to play, and Jan Caspol slowly sat down again.

The air palpitated to the sound of a chord. The sound faded and a dazzling array of electronic melodies moved in some subtle sympathy with its memory. The organ announced another motif, which was then modified, and repeated in scarcely recognizable forms through a series of oscillators.

It was as if the organist spelled out the word which was then seized upon by unseen craftsmen, like monkish scribes in a cloister illuminating holy script with fronds and curlicues on uterine vellum.

The music pierced him with an indescribable sweetness, but at the same time it created a yearning for something else which was so strong it was almost beyond enduring. Each time a fresh musical phrase reached his ear he thought the yearning had been satisfied, and then each time the yearning returned with greater strength than before.

It was like watching an incredibly beautiful structure being built. Each stone seemed to possess a finished perfection in itself, and yet each stone was no more than another step towards that final, unknowable perfection, which would always remain a half-glimpsed dream unless some unimaginably perfect key-stone could be found.

Suddenly the skin on the back of Jan Caspol's neck started to crawl, and he gripped the sides of his chair until the knuckles shone white.

Slowly, gradually, unnoticed at first, as imperceptible as the beginning of love, a new sound had insinuated itself into the woven melody. The new sound assembled the other sounds around itself, binding them to its will, organizing them, creating a new totality of feeling which swelled inside him, making him want to shout, and laugh, and cry.

It was the girl's voice.

Jan Caspol lost all sense of time. It might have been ten minutes, ten hours, or ten years. He listened unblinking, almost without breathing. It wasn't until he became aware of the pain in his back, and in his clenched fingers, that he realized he was surrounded by silence.

Like a man clawing his way back to consciousness he saw the girl, with cropped brown hair, downcast eyes, and a long, clumsy stride, leave the platform and go out through the red velvet curtain in the wall.

When he stood up he was trembling. He made his way with unseeing eyes out of the room, down the precipitous stairs, and into the dark tunnel of Tubal Lane.

15

JAN CASPOL CLEARED the display screen and leaned back in his swivel chair.

The Queen's pregnancy had been confirmed, and her advisers were objecting to gene surgery. The situation held every promise of a first-rate row. Apart from that the news was completely humdrum, and it had been the usual uneventful morning.

Jan leaned back, luxuriating in the termination of his morning discipline. It was a relief to open his mind, like a lock gate, to the flooding memories of the previous evening.

He could scarcely credit his memory as the record of a true experience. The girl at the Fiesta Club had actually been playing tunes and singing songs which he had never heard before. That could only mean that somewhere in Tcity the creative instinct was still alive. There were still people who were capable of producing 'works of art'.

Jan closed his eyes, and decided that he would replay the music in his audio memory until Bendix arrived. But the video buzzed, and Phillippa's face appeared on the screen.

'Good morning, Jan.'

The memories drained away. 'Hello, Phillippa. Trouble?'

'Sort of.'

'Don't tell me.' He was suddenly depressed. 'There's something the matter with Henry?'

'No, no. Henry's all right. He'll do his stuff.'

Jan banished a painful mental picture of himself taking Bendix round the works. 'That's a relief. What's the matter?'

Phillippa was silent. He noticed that her hair had been swept back in untidy strands from her curved, Florentine brow, and there were blue patches under her eyes. It struck him that she looked ill.

''What's the matter, Phillippa?'

'It's nothing to do with the job.'

'What is it?' he asked, kindly.

She bit her lip. 'I'd like to talk to you.'

'Fire away.'

'I mean I'd like to come over to see you.'

Jan looked at her sombre, brooding eyes. 'Of course.'

'I know you're expecting a visitor,' she said. 'What about 1500?'

'That's fine. I'll expect you then.'

Phillippa cleared, and Jan was left to ponder on what her personal trouble might be. But memories of the previous evening intruded, and walking through them with long, clumsy strides was a girl with cropped brown hair and downcast eyes.

He wasn't left to his own thoughts for long.

The triple chimes of the door bell sounded, the second note a fifth under the first, with the third note split and attenuating in a blur of upper harmonics. The chimes represented a phrase taken from the allegro (flute, violin, and electronic tracks) of the 1,374th symphony by Raphael

Rozier, the last composer of the Pre-Denaissance Period.

Glancing at the one-way video as he rose to his feet, Jan saw the expectant face and protuberant eyeballs of Bendix. He went into the hall, and greeted the fleshly original with a welcoming smile.

'Come through, David,' he said. 'Come through.'

Jan led the way through the thickly carpeted hall, and during this brief interval they supported themselves on the traditional talking sticks of their race.

'Well, Jan, what do you think about the way the isobars are moving this morning?'

Jan's face registered that serious concern which such questions had provoked in English minds for centuries.

'If you can believe everything you read in the satellite reports', he said, 'we won't feel more than the edge of the anticyclone.'

Jan stood aside, and followed Bendix into the cocktail lounge, at the far end of which there was an elegant table loaded with bottles and a variety of glasses. Bendix said he would prefer a manzanilla. Jan selected the bottle and poured two drinks.

Stahlex Corporation protocol demanded that on occasions such as this, all drinks should be poured by hand. It was supposed to give the customer the impression that his requirements would always be accommodated, no matter how much trouble it caused the Executives.

Jan almost opened his mouth to quote Hemingway's views on manzanilla, but remembered in time that Bendix didn't like American literature and so he talked about Sanlúcar de Barrameda instead.

Bendix, drink in hand, started to patrol the room, and stopped before a small, framed facsimile taken from the *Historia Ecclesiastica* of Bede. He scrutinized the Latin text, which described how the angel visited Caedmon at Whitby, and began to translate.

' "Caedmon, sing me something," ' translated Bendix. ' "He answered 'I cannot sing and for this cause I left the feast.' Yet said the divine visitant 'You must sing to me.' 'What shall I sing?' asked Caedmon. 'Sing,' the other replied, 'The beginning of created things.' At once Caedmon began a hymn in praise of the Creation, and when he awoke he remembered it." '

Bendix turned to face Jan. 'The first of the English poets,' he added.

Jan nodded. With one part of his mind he was remembering a different singer. With another part of his mind he was tempted to observe that Caedmon was the only poet ever produced by the North East, and that even then it had to be by divine intervention, but he thought it better to refrain. Caedmon's hymn had certainly been a false dawn.

Bendix moved on to the next picture. It showed Durham cathedral in the days when it stood in a loop of the river Wear, before it was dismantled stone by stone and rebuilt on the north bank of the Colorado River. The edifice which had been half church of God, half castle against the Scots, now gazed with blind eyes across Californian desert towards the more recent barbarism of Los Angeles and Pasadena.

The association of ideas provoked Bendix's next comment. 'Mr Steinberg is American, isn't he?'

'Yes', Jan replied. 'Of course.'

'Rather unfortunate with his children, I believe?'

Jan didn't want to say anything, but Bendix was waiting. 'I believe the first child was a boy,' he replied. 'I haven't any details, but apparently Mr Steinberg omitted to arrange for gene surgery, and consequently lost him.'

'I was less interested', said Bendix, 'in Steinberg's attempted assumption of the royal prerogative, than in the character of his daughter. The rumour is, to put it mildly, that she's quite without principles of any kind.'

'They say she's a little wild,' Jan said.

'But I understand that she spends most of her time at unspeakable places in the northern sectors, and that she practises robotomy. Surely such things are undesirable in the City Executive?'

'I think Val Steinberg is much maligned,' Jan lied.

Jan knew that Steinberg had been forced to arrogate his daughter's authority, so that when necessary he could himself operate the city support systems. To change the subject he moved towards the next picture, and Bendix followed.

It was a print showing some kind of artisan family group. The men looked coarse and rough-handed.

'The Stephensons,' Bendix announced. 'The young man with the clay pipe is Robert Stephenson, the greatest engineer of his day.'

Jan began to congratulate himself on the way he'd matched his guest's personality profile.

'But what have we here?' asked Bendix, pausing in front of the next picture. 'A picture of some ancient works?'

'Yes. It's—'

'No.' Bendix held up his hand. 'Let me guess.'

Bendix sipped his pale drink as he examined the picture. Jan looked over his shoulder at the two blast furnaces, a sovereign pair wearing tangled crowns of gas offtakes and downcomers, with adjacent rows of hot blast stoves standing by like attendant pages.

'I don't know much about industrial archaeology', said Bendix, 'but I think it's a steel works. I'll guess that it's Dorman Long.'

'Very nearly,' Jan said, apologetically. 'Actually it's the Hartlepool works of the South Durham Steel and Iron Company. Mr Steinberg's house is virtually on the site where the coke ovens used to be.'

'Really?'

Bendix left the pictures and returned to the table on which the bottles stood. Jan saw him smile, and knew that he'd now recognized the table as the work of Sheraton. He also knew that it would be quite superfluous to mention that Sheraton was a native of what was now the Second Sector.

'Another drink, David?'

'Just a small one, thanks.'

The selected environment had obviously mellowed Bendix. To Jan the assorted Northumbriana of the cocktail lounge seemed little enough to show for one and a half thousand years of history between the Tyne and the Tees, but they had done the trick.

'Your pictures tell me something about you, Jan,' Bendix said, sipping his second manzanilla.

'What's that?'

'Your pictures represent events in a chronological order, although spatial relationships would have dictated a different sequence.'

'Well?'

'I would say you were a man who had an almost painful awareness of the discontinuity of the past. You therefore strive to impose some sort of continuity upon it, so that you can look backwards and feel that you have somehow grown out of it, and that you have a relationship with it.'

Jan Caspol was surprised at the insight, but he laughed. 'Do you know what, David? I think you may well have something there.'

'And yet look at the picture of that old steel works,' said Bendix. 'Can you honestly feel that you have grown out of that?'

'Yes, I can.' Jan was serious. 'That was one of the satisfying things about the iron and steel industry. Behind the men who worked in it there were the Roman bloomeries, the ancient forests which the Spanish Armada tried to burn, the exploitation of the coal fields. Merely to walk through a rolling mill was to become part of an unfolding flux of events, to feel you were sailing on a huge river of ingenuity in the manipulation of metal, and that . . . but my dear David, I am talking too much.'

'On the contrary. But you seem to have missed my point.'

'In any case,' Jan said, touching his arm, 'we can continue our discussion over lunch.'

16

BENDIX PUSHED HIS SOUP DISH, now emptied of chicken velouté, towards the return chute.

'You were observing,' he said, 'that when a man worked in a steel rolling mill he felt himself, in some mysterious way, linked to everything which had gone before.'

'That's my belief,' said Jan. 'Service *à la russe*,' he added, as he thumbed the button which brought forward Meissen plates with the entrées, comprising boned quails stuffed with forcemeats of calves' liver, foie gras and truffles, all liberally sprinkled with brandy.

Jan poured some wine. Bendix sniffed, tasted, and looked at the bottle. The bottle was turned so that the label was on the other side.

'What do you think of the wine?' asked Jan.

'Excellent. But I can't quite place it.'

Bendix held his glass high, and scrutinized the colour as he rotated it against the light. Then he brought the glass to his nose once more, and sniffed audibly two or three times.

'It's obviously a claret,' he said. 'And a good one.'

Bendix took a small sip, which he held in the front of his mouth against his teeth, so that he could test for sourness with the tip of his tongue. When that exercise had been completed he tilted his head back slightly and inhaled deeply, to savour the bouquet and measure the ethers and aldehydes. The wine spread over the flat of his tongue, where he was able to register the body, smoothness, and texture. After that Bendix rolled the sample against his cheeks and under his tongue to check for bitterness.

Finally Bendix swallowed slowly and deliberately, with mouth and eyes firmly closed, and waited perhaps ten seconds for the full perfume of the aftertaste.

Bendix opened his eyes. 'As I said, it's a claret, and it's from the Médoc, but I still can't place it. Too much body for St Julien, too much bouquet for Margaux, and yet not quite big enough for St Estèphe or Pauillac. I honestly don't know. All I can say is that it's from one of the classic communes.'

Jan chuckled delightedly. 'In fact it's from Listrac.'

'Listrac!' Bendix was astounded, and the whites of his protuberant eyes appeared round the full circumference of each iris. 'Listrac! I didn't think any of their wines were this good. There's only Fourcas-Dupré in the present classification, and I didn't think Listrac had even a fifth cru in the old classification of 1855.'

'That's right.' Jan nodded over his quails. 'The Stahlex Corporation was a late starter in the scramble for vineyards. The Rothschilds were the first, by a long margin, and they put their five arrows on the weathercock at Château Lafite about 200 years before we even started to look around.'

'Perhaps you were so late', Bendix suggested, 'because people in heavy industry have traditionally been drinkers of strong beer.'

'Perhaps,' agreed Jan. 'But whatever the reason, when we entered the market all the grands crus had been snapped up years before. So we made an exhaustive survey, and decided that Château Joinville-Robert, at Listrac, was grossly undervalued and had good potential. A new vigneron, some years of selective weather control, and some further years in bottle, have produced the wine you are drinking.'

Jan turned the bottle.

Bendix finished chewing some quail and nodded towards the label. 'I hope you're not going to tell me that the only way to taste Château Stahlex-Joinville-Robert is to be entertained by the Stahlex Corporation?'

'I must admit,' Jan said, 'that you would normally see only the poorer years outside the Corporation. Don't forget, David, that the château has to supply not only ourselves, but also our colleagues at Bremerhaven, Dunkirk, and Brindisi, as well as our American plants. You know how the Americans undervalue their own wines, even now.'

'Running a vineyard must be an expensive business?'

'I suppose it is. Grape-pickers are paid almost as highly as barbers.'

Bendix moved his plate aside, and pushed his glass forward to receive some more wine. 'But we were talking, I think, about the sense of continuity in the steel industry.'

'Yes, I'm sorry, David. I interrupted your train of thought.'

'Not at all,' Bendix protested. 'It's simply that I

don't understand what you mean.'

'What I mean', said Jan, 'is that the steelworker felt himself to be part of a long chain of events, because he was unconsciously aware that what he actually did grew naturally out of the work of previous centuries, and the innovations of men like Sturtevant, Darby, Cort, Bessemer, Siemens, Thomas and Gilchrist, Hadfield, Morgan—'

Bendix finished his wine. 'But that doesn't make the steel industry unique.'

Jan thumbed the main course: Rouen duckling, its red flesh testifying to death by smothering instead of bleeding, cooked with Madeira and stoned Morella cherries.

'Let's consider this excellent meal,' continued Bendix. 'You could argue that we are taking part in an ancient ritual that has been modified by the innovations of Catherine of Medici, La Varenne, Vincent de la Chapelle, Laguipière, Brillat-Savarin, and Grimod de la Reynière.'

Jan poured from the second bottle. 'Of course. In fact you can push the analogy further back, through Lucullus and Apicius, beyond Sardanapalus, until everything is lost in savagery, and you reach the point when someone made the first iron pot and boiled the first stew in it.'

'If you think the first iron worker was the first cook', laughed Bendix, 'then I won't argue with you.'

'The same family, anyway,' Jan said.

Bendix forked his duckling, and looked at the label on the second bottle. It said *Richebourg, 18416 Bouteilles Récoltées, No 01093, Année 2095*.

'How on earth did you get hold of this?' asked Bendix, sipping the wine. 'I thought Richebourg was brought up long ago.'

'That is true. GK bought it from the *Société Civile de la Romanée-Conti,* and so I have to trade bottles with them. They insist on three bottles of Stahlex-Joinville-Robert for one of Richebourg. It sounds like a hard bargain, but I think it's fair enough when you think of the size of GK and remember that Richebourg has only just over eight hectares.'

Bendix seemed disposed to eat without talking for a while. Jan moved a finger control under the table, and the cello in Mozart's Prussian Quartets began to caress the air with a greater plangency.

With a sigh Bendix laid down his knife and fork and sat back. 'I grant you that the steel worker might have had a deeply satisfying sense of identity with history, but as I said before over sherry, I think you've missed the point.'

'What's that?'

'The industry you are talking about has disappeared.'

Jan leaned forward. 'The industry hasn't disappeared. It still exists. Just as it continued to exist when steel replaced iron, so it still exists in our own day, when stahlex has replaced steel and virtually everything else besides.'

Bendix tried to refuse anything further to eat, but was persuaded to pick at some *mille-feuille*, which were exact replicas of those which Carême used to make for Talleyrand.

'You really think so?' he asked.

'Yes. I do. When the multi-stage fluid bed reactor replaced the blast furnace, and when you could convert steel in a counter flow shaft and withdraw it by vacuum extraction, and when continuous casting had eliminated rolling mills . . . in other words when steel had become a process industry, which it was before the end of the 20th century, you already had the seeds of the stahlex industry you have today.'

'So the iron and steel industry,' commented Bendix, 'was reborn from its own ashes, like the Phoenix?'

'Precisely.'

Bendix pondered, warming a glass of champagne brandy in his hand. 'But what about the great army of steel workers?' he said. 'The men with the deeply satisfying sense of identity. You can't deny that they've all disappeared.'

'Of course they have.' Jan had difficulty in hiding his impatience at the childishness of the observation. 'It's part of the same natural development.'

17

AT 1500 PRECISELY the triple chimes sounded again, and the upper harmonics of the third note were still dancing in the air when Phillippa came in. She looked pale and nervous as she settled herself on the edge of a chair. With a shake of her head she refused a drink, but accepted a felicity.

Jan gave her a light. 'If you're in some kind of trouble, Phillippa, and you want help, you've only got to ask.'

'It's a bit difficult for me to begin,' she said.

'Try.'

She sucked at her felicity and inhaled deeply. 'You go into the city quite frequently,' she said, through the mauve smoke.

'Now and again.' He was mystified.

'With Nick?'

'Sometimes.' As he said it he knew that tonight he would go into the city alone.

'What do you do?' she asked. 'Don't tell me it's to get your hair cut.'

Jan laughed at the old joke, but her features didn't relax.

'If Nick and I have arranged to go in together', he said, more seriously, 'we usually meet in the Seaton Hotel and have a few drinks there. Then we take the autos, and have a drink at the Gatehouse.'

'By which time I imagine you're both rather the worse for wear.'

Jan pulled a wry face. 'Remember it's the last drink we can have, apart from anything we take into the city with us.'

'All right. Go on.'

'Well,' Jan waved his arm vaguely. 'We struggle about in the streets, rubbing shoulders with the people, as it were.'

'What about entertainment?'

'We might go to a club or two. The Fun Palace and the Blue Star, usually.'

'And what's there?'

'People mainly. There's music of a kind, but nothing earlier than Raphael Rozier. Perhaps a bit of a floor show.'

'What does the floor show consist of?' pursued Phillippa.

Jan waved his arm vaguely again. 'You know the sort of things. Autocrooners. Occasionally some gimmickry of Gerry Peters. Those sorts of things.'

'Presumably the crooners are always robots,' she said, 'without exception.'

'Presumably.'

'And then what do you do?'

But Jan's thoughts had been diverted by the memory of the only exception he'd ever come across. He recalled the soft voice, the brown hair, the downcast eyes.

'And then what do you do?' she repeated.

'I usually come home.'

'Straight away?'

'As a rule.' Jan was on the defensive. 'If it's getting near the Curfew, of course, you've got to stay over until everything has stopped.'

'And Nick?'

'He more or less does the same.'

She stared into his face. 'But you take both autos in case you get separated by the entertainment available.'

'It's more convenient,' he said. 'As you say, we might get separated in the crowds. But look here, Phillippa, I wish you'd tell me what you're driving at.'

She inhaled heavily, and flicked her half-finished felicity into the atomizer where it disappeared with a yellow flash. Painfully twisting her interlaced fingers, she stared blindly at some point on the floor, and then looked at him with clouded eyes.

'Tell me about the aphrodollies,' she said.

Jan shifted his position uneasily, not liking the course the conversation had taken. 'You must know something about them. Girls who think they're suitable apply to the aphrocollege. They are screened for gestalt, and most of them are rejected at once. The girls who get through the screening are given physiological examinations, which are mainly concerned with vaso-motor controls and glandular secretions. Once again, most of them are rejected, and the remainder are subjected to batteries of psychological tests. The small number who finally get through are given two years of mental and physical conditioning before they pass out as full graduates.'

'What form does the physical conditioning take?'

Jan wanted to avoid the question. 'I don't really know much about it.'

'Tell me,' she said. 'I want to know.'

'It's not the kind of thing people talk about,' he

replied. 'They increase the strength of the restrictor muscles, and so on.'

'I see,' said Phillippa, with sudden bitterness. 'It's the kind of thing you close your mind to. It's the manure that nurtures the flower.'

He was startled by the new tone in her voice. 'What's the matter?' he asked, softly.

'You go home with an aphrodolly now and again, don't you, Jan?'

'Now and again,' he admitted.

'And Nick rather more frequently.'

He wasn't sure whether it was a question, and he didn't try to answer it. With a feeling of immense unhappiness he began to anticipate what was to come.

'I imagine,' she continued, 'that they are what you call *good*. I suppose it's quite an experience for those who can afford it.'

'I suppose so.'

'Then tell me this. Can a man who is used to aphrodollies be content with an . . . an ordinary woman, provided she . . . ' Without warning Phillippa's voice choked into a sob, but she got it under control almost immediately. '. . . provided she loves him?'

Jan Caspol sprang impulsively from his chair, and squeezed her shoulders with his hands. Turning away he punched out two whiskies, placed one in her hand, and gave her another felicity.

'It is possible,' he said. 'Believe me Phillippa, I *know* it's possible.'

She was too full of her own misery to notice the personal revelation implied in his statement.

'It's Nick, isn't it?' he asked quietly.

She nodded, averting her eyes and sipping the whisky.

Jan was intensely sorry for her. It was bad luck for Phillippa, but it was only to be expected. Nick had always been a nucleus around which women orbited in complex but predetermined paths like captive electrons in a Niels Bohr atom. Even Val Steinberg had been involved with Nick for a short period, and Jan sometimes wondered how much of Val's desperate search for some sort of happiness was attributable to that fact.

'I love him to the point of despair,' Phillippa said in an almost inaudible voice. 'I would suffer any humility to hold him in my arms.'

Jan didn't know what to say.

Phillippa tried to adopt a hard, bright tone, which made Jan's heart ache. 'It's strange, isn't it,' she continued, 'that we should have made ourselves so clever, with our artificially enhanced intelligence and memories with total recall, and yet we suffer the same emotional weaknesses as the pastoral shepherds and nymphs of Syracusan poetry. Bion and Moschus would understand us better than we do ourselves.'

He smiled. 'Exactly so, Phillippa.'

She swallowed some more whisky, and tried to return the smile.

'Does Nick know?' he asked.

'Yes. He knows.'

Jan looked at her face. The blonde hair was swept back from her tall brow, so as to hide the surgical scars, and it was richly braided behind her head. With her slim, elegant figure, and her small breasts, he wondered whether she consciously aped the Florentine ideal of the cinquecento. But she was no Simonetta Vespucci. And although Botticelli might have loved her, it was unlikely that Nick Levantine ever would.

'I'm sorry, Phillippa. I really am. It's difficult to see what I can do, but if I ever can help you I shall.'

She flicked her felicity into the atomizer, gulped her whisky, and stood up. 'Thank you, Jan. I know there's nothing you can do. I only hope you don't think me too stupid for talking about it.'

'Not a bit.'

'My coming here and telling you my troubles is about as useful as a Coptic prayer against locusts. But I had to talk to somebody, and you . . . "

'Of course,' said Jan, as he followed her to the door. 'If it makes you feel any better, remember that this is something that everybody goes through some time or other.'

'I'm familiar with all the consolations of philosophy. None of them will cure my tooth-ache.'

She turned at the door.

'One thought does console me,' she added.

'Yes?'

Her face was lined with pain as she spoke. 'I cannot believe that a love as strong as mine can't alter the nature of things. I can't help believing that one day soon I shall put my arms around him, and he will not resist.'

Phillippa turned to go, and left Jan with his own thoughts, his own memories.

18

THE AUTO CRUISED down a long straight road, with trees on each side. The pre-punched co-ordinates brought it to a halt in the works auto-park, and Bendix stepped out.

Before him was an ornamental stahlex gate, which swung open at his approach. He found him-self in a narrow avenue, overhung with the branches of trees and surrounded by the songs of birds. At the other end of the avenue a figure had appeared.

Henry was walking towards him with a mea-sured stride, and his arms diverged slightly from his sides with the palms turned frontwards in a histrionic gesture of welcome. His unblinking eyes shone like friendly beacons.

The GK Series 7B could be adapted for a wide variety of industrial applications, and they made ideal mystagogues. In addition, Henry had been provided with a thermoplastic face, and the cor-ners of his eyes were crinkly like those of the heroes in computer-generated women's fiction.

'Welcome to the British works of the Stahlex Corporation,' he called, while he was still some distance away.

Henry advanced steadily until Bendix came up to him. Then the robot turned through 180 degrees and began to retrace his steps at an easy pace.

'The trees which overhang our path are Cedars of Lebanon,' he said. 'You will notice that the branches, at first ascending, become horizontal further from the trunk . . .'

Bendix wasn't interested in the flora and fauna, but Henry chatted away nevertheless, pointing with his unjointed index finger at items considered worthy of remark, and pausing for questions which never came.

At the end of the avenue Henry halted, and pointed once again. 'Those extremely tall trees are Douglas Firs,' he said, in his pre-recorded voice. 'They rise to a height of over 70 metres, and we are particularly proud of them.'

Henry moved to the right, and they came upon a guide car standing on narrow gauge rails. Bendix got inside, and sat down with a feeling of relief. He had dined slightly too well for comfort. Henry climbed in after him, and closed the bubble roof.

'We are going on the standard works tour', Henry announced, 'and there will be a general commentary throughout the trip from the car's speaker unit. If at any point you require further information, all you have to do is press the button at your elbow. The guide car will stop, and I shall take over and answer any questions you wish to put. Have you any questions before we start?'

'No,' said Bendix.

The guide car rolled away between the trees on its narrow gauge railway. Henry was perfectly immobile now, as if wishing to efface himself completely, but Bendix was determined to miss no detail offered by the uninterrupted vision of the bubble roof.

They rounded a corner and a large rectangular building came into view. The speaker unit crackled into life.

> *You are looking at the first unit in the Metals Plant. Metal scrap is continuously tipped into a shredding machine which contains pulsed scanning lasers. The shredded metal is conveyed to a liquefier, which is effectively a continuous electric induction furnace.*

The guide car skirted the shredding machine, and began to approach the first of a series of colossal, silvery spheres. The spheres had enormous cooling fins upon their exterior, and the air surrounding them shimmered with heat.

> *These spherical containers hold the metallic input in liquid form. The containers are jackets by layers of circulating liquid potassium, which now transfers the heat which it has absorbed as a reactor coolant. The storage chambers are purged continuously with hydrogen from the electrolysis plant which you will see later. The hydrogen eliminates oxygen from the metallic fluid, and provides a stirring action at the same time.*

Bendix pressed the stop button, and the guide car halted between the first and second spheres. Henry's circuits snapped on, and he turned his eyes upon the passenger.

'I want to ask some questions about heat disposal,' Bendix said.

'Please do.'

'Presumably surplus heat not required in the works is diverted to other uses.'

'Yes,' Henry replied. 'The works provides all the heat requirements of Tcity. Any further surplus for which there is no alternative use is radiated away as you see, and sunk at various points in the works.'

Bendix wiped his forehead. 'Might not fluctuations in demand for stahlex overload your heat-sinking facilities?'

'No. There are only very small fluctuations in the demand for stahlex, and they are always anticipated in the sales forecast. The heat-sinking facilities are more than adequate to compensate for such variations.'

'But what if there *was* a large, unexpected change in demand,' Bendix insisted, and a drop of sweat ran off the end of his nose. 'What would happen then?'

There was an almost imperceptible pause as Henry located a hitherto unused portion of his data banks. 'A storage sphere would be taken off stream, or a spare one put into commission, as the case may be, in order to balance the required throughputs and remain within the safety parameters. But these eventualities are so unlikely that they can be disregarded.'

'But if a sphere was taken off stream', persisted Bendix, 'wouldn't there be a danger of—'

The guide car started to roll forward.

'Hey!' Bendix shouted. 'Just a minute!'

The car speaker intervened.

We are profoundly sorry that we must override your request and move on. We had waited the maximum permissible period at the storage spheres, and any further delay would have resulted in damage by heat to the vehicle and consequently to the occupants.

Henry looked at Bendix with the unwinking eyes of a fish. 'If you would care to make a note of your further questions', he said, 'I should be pleased to answer them at the conclusion of the tour.'

Bendix smiled to himself as the guide car passed the last of the storage spheres, and another structure became visible through the bubble roof. There was no likelihood of his forgetting the other questions.

This is the vaporizer. Fluid metal is drawn from the storage spheres as required and subsequently atomized by an inert helium atmosphere. There are three stages which correspond to the three stages of the fractionator which we are now approaching.

Bendix looked upwards at the massive tower which thrust its gleaming top above the highest trees.

The metal, now in helium vapour, is pumped around the 3-stage fractionator. The Fe is sent to the sputter mills, and the other materials to the by-products unit. The helium is reconstituted for further cycling and lost helium is replaced through homeostatic controls from the electrolysis plant.

Bendix leaned back, and looked directly upwards through the bubble roof. The fractionating column appeared to taper above him like a cathedral spire. It struck him that from the top, on a clear day, it would be possible to see the entire semicircular sweep of the windowless city walls as they embraced the territory of the Executives like the arms of a crescent moon.

The guide car rolled on. Bendix peered out at the by-products unit, and listened to the commentary. This was followed by the power house which contained the fusion reactors. A magnetohydrodynamic generator used the atomized and ionized potassium to produce an electrical output of 2,000 MW with a coolant heat output of 5,000 MW.

The car circled the 500 MW electrolysis plant, which supplied the purging hydrogen and other gases, crossed its previous tracks, and ran through a leafy glade into the Substrate Plant.

> *This is the organic substrate unit. The raw material is desert soil, which is brought by subterranean conveyors from the limitless reserves of the North Sea beaches. The unit produces 1-, 2-, and 3-D substrates of extreme purity, but with a crystal structure which at this stage is only partially organized.*

The narrow gauge railway carried the guide car to a building of cyclopean proportions, and as it began to roll past, the speaker unit resumed its commentary.

> *You now see the substrate layering building, where a series of heating, ultrasonic, and elec-*

*tric treatments produce substrates in the form
required for interfacing. When they leave this
building the substrates have a uniform and
exact crystal structure, and are ready for the
sputter mills.*

The car left the Substrate Plant, crossed its
tracks once more, and re-entered the trees. Henry
perked up, and looked at Bendix with earnest,
unblinking eyes.

'These extremely tall trees are the Douglas Firs
I pointed out before,' he said. 'The Douglas Fir is a
native of North America, where it—'

'Keep quiet about trees,' snapped Bendix. 'As
soon as we have a minute to spare I want to ask my
further questions about the heat-sinking facilities.'

Henry didn't bat an eyelid. 'I am sorry. I
thought a few more words about the trees might
occupy this brief interval. As it is, I'm afraid there
isn't sufficient time to—'

The speaker unit interrupted.

*We are now approaching the sputter mills,
where materials from the Metals Plant and
the Substrate Plant are brought together and
interfaced to form stahlex. The first building
is the Sheet Sputter Mill, where 2-D substrate
sheets are placed in vacuum chambers and
sputtered with vaporized Fe under controlled
conditions. The layer of Fe will be 2, 3, or 4
molecules thick, according to customer
specification. The sputtered sheets are then
recirculated on air cushioned beds to form
sandwiches of varying thickness, in which the
Fe/substrate layers all interlock perfectly at
the interfaces through their matching crystalline structure. The number of lay–*

Bendix pressed the button impatiently. The guide car halted, and the commentary stopped in mid-word.

'Do you have a question about the sputter mills?' asked Henry.

'I have,' Bendix said irritably. 'Do they all work on the same principle?'

'Yes. They employ the same principle to make different stahlex shapes. We have a sheet mill, a block mill, a—'

'In that case,' said Bendix, 'you can take me back to the autopark.'

'What about edge-finishing, surface treatment, and inspection monitoring?'

'No.'

'Would you like to see the automatic loading to the independent monorail systems, which run out through the city walls and—'

'No,' shouted Bendix. 'Take me back to the autopark immediately.'

Henry issued an overriding command, and the guide car started to reverse silently along the route by which it had come.

'Would you now like to ask your further question about heat-sinking?' asked Henry.

Bendix grimly extracted a writing pad and a stylo. 'If you don't mind,' he said.

19

THE MAN WITH the Sicilian moustache looked up, and removed the tooth-pick from his mouth. Jan paid his money, crossed the brightly lit ante-room, and entered the club.

He strained his eyes around the darkened room, glancing at each shadowy figure in turn, but could see no sign of the girl. Reminding himself that he was a little earlier than on the previous evening, he decided to kill time by going over to the dimly lit bar in the wall.

The bar was a fascinating piece of reconstruction, and he leaned his elbows on the counter to survey it. On the wall behind the bar there was an engraved mirror, and on its uneven surface he saw his own distorted face, and indistinct, gloomy shapes flitting like phantoms in the candle-lit room behind him.

Jan sensed that the girl was near him, and turned. On his left a suspended light shed a feeble glow over the tiny floor space reserved for dancing. Beyond that was the raised platform on which the antique organ stood, wreathed in shadows and silence. He cast his eyes round the rest of the room, and returned his attention to the bar.

Below the engraved mirror dummy bottles of beer were arranged horizontally in racks, and their nozzles protruded like uncovered cannon from the sides of a man-o'-war. It was strange, he reflected, how people liked to pretend that things hadn't changed all that much.

A music generator suddenly made the air vibrate with a series of sine notes. The absence of overtones deprived the notes of timbre, making them dull and flat. An electronic chord was shivered in a reverberator, and then a mechanical voice began to wail.

> *a new venus*
> *arose*
> *from the alien*
> *waves*
> *of ammoniac*
> *snows*
> *which swirl round*
> *Jupiter*
> *for ever*
> *and ever*
> *and ever*

Jan looked up, and saw that there was now another face in the mirror, near to his own. The light was poor, and the mirror was defective and not well polished, but the face clutched at him like a memory. He almost feared that she wasn't really there, and he continued to stare at her reflection, as if he wasn't sure of the substance but was determined to grasp the shadow.

The ululation filled the room.

> *each breast is*
> *a twin*
> *of silver*
> *light*
> *like the stars which*
> *spin*
> *and eclipse*
> *in Perseus*
> *for ever*
> *and ever*
> *and ever*

He turned, and there she was with her oval face framed by soft, brown hair. Her small nose was slightly freckled by the artificial suns of the thruways. And now he was seeing her eyes for the first time, and they were a colour he'd never seen before. Or more truthfully, he thought, her eyes were a mixture of colours which changed when she moved her head slightly—grey, green, blue.

The thought crossed his mind that her eyes were coloured like the backs of freshly caught mackerel, and the thought made him want to laugh.

'Would you like a drink?' he asked.

'Thank you. I'll have a fruit juice. Any fruit juice.'

Her voice was soft, and went over him like a caress. His hand trembled as he punched the order.

Jan watched her as she put the glass to her mouth, and her top lip pouted over the rim. She knew that he was looking at her, and lowered her eyes. The light from the bar shone directly on her face. A network of delicate blue veins made her rounded eyelids look like bridle-path systems on adjacent hills, reproduced on small scale maps, or viewed from an ornithopter on a bright, sunny day.

He gestured towards the tables. 'Should we sit down?'

Her lip sucked softly at the rim as she removed the glass. 'Yes. But aren't you going to have a drink?'

'Of course.'

He punched a small glass of beer for himself, and led the way to the nearest table. They sat opposite each other, with the light of a flickering candle between them.

'What's your name?' he asked.

'Meriol. Meriol Stavanger.'

The mechanical voice screeched out its synthetic lusts.

> *of galactic*
> *mist*
> *her thighs*
> *are made*
> *and when she*
> *kissed*
> *my heart was*
> *hers*
> *for ever*
> *and ever*
> *and ever*

The last phrase of the song bounced backwards and forwards in an echo chamber, until it decayed and died into silence. Then a new rhythm of percussive sound disturbed the atmosphere.

Jan placed his untasted drink on the table. 'Should we dance?'

She stood up without a word, and made her way between the tables towards the diminutive dance floor. Jan followed her, and as Meriol entered the pool of light he looked at her slim waist and her tapered legs. Then she turned round, and smiled while she waited for him.

Jan held her close as they moved to the music and the rounded contours of her hips filled the palms of his hands like a double blessing. He looked down. Meriol lifted her face, and those extraordinary eyes regarded him steadily.

'You play the organ and sing,' he said.

She blushed faintly. 'Yes.'

'It's amazing.'

Meriol lowered her face against him, and he could see nothing except her soft hair and the pink tips of her ears.

The rhythm of the music changed.

'Let's sit down,' he said.

They left the floor, and returned to their table. Jan moved the Vat 69 bottle to one side so that he could see her better. The unsteady flame of the candle in the bottle threw moving shadows across her face. He watched the candle-light licking at her eyelids, her small freckled nose, the lobes of her ears, and he saw the darkness come and go under her bottom lip.

A strange excitement filled him, growing and swelling inside him, straining against all the arterial doors in his body, effervescing, like sparkling wine trapped and stoppered in a bottle.

He pretended to sip his beer.

'I must go now,' she said.

Jan lowered his glass, and reached across the table with his other hand to seize her fingers.

'Why?'

All the other women he'd ever met, ever known, were nothing now. All his memories of kisses and caresses, of making love in cruising autos and in aphrodomes and aphrocells, were shadows only, dim reflections of unimportant things, like unimportant photographs of unimportant places and of people whose names he'd forgotten, photographs of places and people which seemed important at the time, but which were now empty and meaningless, because their associations had fled.

'Because I've got to sing,' she said.

He was relieved. 'But must you go now?'

'Yes.'

Meriol sat tensely, with her fingers imprisoned in his hand.

'How long will you be singing?'

'I don't know.'

'I'll wait,' he said. 'But don't be too long.'

She said nothing, and he squeezed her fingers.

'Don't be too long,' he repeated. 'You won't be very long, will you?'

Meriol smiled slightly. 'Why? Don't you like to hear me sing?'

'Of course I do,' he said, with some violence. 'More than anything else in the world. It's just that I . . . I sat and listened to you last night.'

'I know you did.' She smiled to herself, almost secretly. 'I remember you did.'

Meriol stood up, but he kept hold of her hand.

'I'm waiting,' he said, 'partly because I want to hear you sing, and partly . . . ' He laughed. 'My name's Jan Caspol,' he added.

She turned her head away, and slowly withdrew her hand. Jan watched her make her way through the tables once more, cross the small dance floor, and mount the platform to sit behind the organ.

Meriol began to play, and her voice sucked at his heart.

20

THE PEOPLE BEGAN to leave in ones and twos. A group of three went out together, and quite suddenly the club had a deserted air. The music generator was switched on again, and its scrambled notes buzzed around the room like maddened flies.

Jan Caspol stretched his legs under the table and marvelled at the unreality of his experience.

Meriol had kept her head down while she was playing, and when she sang she turned towards a microphone on a stand by her side. She had looked up only now and again, with eyes that were questioning, almost frightened, and when she discovered he was still gazing at her she had smiled tremulously and looked away.

When Meriol left the platform she had crossed with long strides, eyes lowered, to the red velvet curtain in the side wall. Jan waited for her, his nerves still tingling with the memory of her voice.

The processed music began to fade and then terminated with a click. The man from the pay desk came in, looked around, and saw Jan. He removed the tooth-pick from his mouth as if to speak, but changed his mind and went out.

The club room was as silent as a forgotten catacomb. Jan looked about him, at the automatic bar with its unpolished mirror, at the silhouette of the organ, at the unmoving velvet curtain through which Meriol had disappeared, at her glass of fruit juice, and his own untouched beer. A feeling of apprehension started to uncurl in his stomach.

The moustached man came in again, and began to move around the tables, emptying ash trays into a large bag. He looked up once or twice, but didn't speak until he reached Jan's table.

'Closed now, sir.'

'I'd just like to wait a few minutes if you don't mind.'

'Everything's finished now, sir.'

The man emptied Jan's ash tray into the bag, as if to enforce his point by a piece of symbolic ritual, and moved on to the next table. Jan felt sick. He tried not to watch the curtain, and told himself that in a moment it would be swept aside, and Meriol would come striding towards him with some perfectly obvious reason for being so long.

'Sorry, sir. I'll have to lock up when I've wiped the tables down.'

Jan looked towards him. 'I'm waiting for Meriol.'

'Meriol!' The man was startled. He straightened up from his work and almost laughed. It appeared that of all the unlikely reasons Jan might have for sitting there, the reason just given was so unlikely as to be beyond belief.

'Yes,' said Jan, with a casualness he didn't feel. 'For Meriol.'

'Meriol! You'll have a long wait for Meriol.'

The man emptied the final ash tray, and carried his bag out into the ante-room. Jan immediately hurried across the floor, and dashed the red curtain aside. Behind it was a door which opened at his touch, and he passed through into a dressing room.

The room was small and shabby, with a door in the opposite wall. A tattered carpet was on the floor, and an old-fashioned sofa was pushed against the wall, with a faded cover and one castor missing. There were a couple of chairs, and a table with a—

Jan Caspol stepped up to the table. On it was a figure formed out of very narrow, fine gauge stahlex strip. It represented a woman, swooning in some kind of agony or ecstasy, with her head thrown back and eyes closed, as if to beg for mercy or beseech some additional favour. Whether the ecstasy was religious or sexual, spiritual of sensual, Jan couldn't tell. It reminded him of Bernini's St Teresa.

He lifted the figure from the table. The artist had used his material with great cunning to capture a moment of rapture in which the experience of the here-and-now spills over into eternity. He turned the figure in his hands to observe the face with its lowered eyelids.

'Excuse me, sir, if you're in the dressing room I must ask you to—'

As soon as Jan heard the voice he crossed the room and tried the door in the wall. The door opened, and presented him with a series of steps which curved upwards out of sight.

He began to ascend, and immediately discovered that he was on a spiral staircase. The walls on both sides of the stairway were blank, but he kept imagining that after the next circle he would come upon a door which in some mysterious, and yet absolutely definite manner, would declare itself as the entrance to Meriol's room.

As he climbed the steps a distant humming noise reached his ears, and after a while he realized it was becoming louder. The stairway continued to curl upwards, but its sides remained without doors or windows or openings of any kind. Round and round the stairway went, upwards and upwards, until he could no longer estimate how far he'd travelled or how high he might be, and the humming noise was insistent in his ears.

Another spiral, and Jan cursed with disappointment as the stairway debouched into the scurrying crowds of a main corridor. There was no option but to obey the luminous waymarks and follow the traffic flow.

While he walked he wondered whether there would be any point in turning off into the next vestibule, but dismissed the idea before it was fully formed. It was futile. Meriol might live in any of the hundreds of vestibules which ran into this corridor or into the adjacent corridors, or she might have taken a levator to any of the hundred floors, or she might have crossed the thruway and entered another beeblock. In fact there was no reason why she mightn't live in a different Sector altogether.

Jan looked up at the waymarks in the ceiling, memorizing the number of the next vestibule on his left and the span of the module numbers it contained. At least he would be able to find the spiral stairway again.

The perfumed ozone blew in his face, mitigating the body odours around him and fanning the hair across his forehead. He was overtaken by an overwhelming sensation of loneliness. Here, where people pressed him on every side, where he could see hundreds upon hundreds of them walking in the same direction, he felt himself to be the only one whose journey hadn't any purpose.

It happened in a further dozen metres.

21

SOMEONE IN FRONT OF HIM had stumbled. Jan saw the slightly built figure lose its footing and spin round under the buffets of the passing crowd. The unfortunate individual would have fallen to the ground immediately, had it not been for the surrounding press of people. As it was he began to sag at the knees, and disappeared from view as Jan forced his way forwards.

It seemed to take a long time to reach the spot. So long, in fact, that for some moments Jan thought he'd lost his bearings, and that he'd passed the fallen man like a ship passing a drowning swimmer. But he saw someone in front of him trip over an unseen obstacle, then recover his balance and walk on, and Jan knew that he was still on beam.

Before he reached the spot Jan decided exactly what he was going to do. He knew that if he hesitated, or stooped and tried to lift the man, he would be knocked headlong by the people who were following.

Another man, directly in front of him, staggered and almost fell over the obstruction, and a moment later Jan found the prostrate form beneath his feet. He immediately moved to the head, plunged his hands under the armpits, and started to walk backwards dragging the body after him.

As he struggled backwards he gazed upon a sea of faces, which belonged to an army of people who appeared determined to overhaul him and trample upon the victim's legs. He continued to haul his burden in the direction of the traffic flow, but all the time he was trying to edge closer to the nearer wall.

The sweat sprang onto Jan Caspol's forehead, where it accumulated in globules and ran down the sides of his nose. Every now and again someone trod on the trailing legs of the unconscious man, abruptly adding to the weight of Jan's load and wrenching his arms in their sockets, so that he would have given anything to be able to drop the body and turn tail.

Slowly, but not very surely, he managed to drag the man to the left-hand wall. Jan looked desperately for a retrieval panel, but could see no sign of one. He continued to drag his burden, keeping as close as possible to the wall, so that he had people on one side only to contend with.

The retrieval panels occurred every 200 metres, and Jan was forced to accept the fact that when he first made contact with the wall he must have just passed one.

The constant bumping of the passers-by who kept knocking him against the wall, the wrenching of his arms, and the aching muscles in his back, became an unbearable torture. He persevered, with the mindless determination of a fallen climber who clings to some painful ledge by his finger tips. His hands began to slip from the man's armpits, and in the same second he found his elbow rubbing over a retrieval panel.

Jan stopped, quickly pushed the unconscious figure into a sitting position, and turned it around so that the feet were pointing in the direction of the traffic flow. Then, Jan stood behind in order to protect the man's head with his body and support the man's back against his knees. That done, he pressed the bright red retrieval button, and concentrated on maintaining his position in the bustling crowd, anchoring himself like a rock against an ebb tide.

Far away, in the direction from which he had come, an intermittent whistle commenced. The whistle was high-pitched and urgent, and Jan sensed a tremor of unease run through the crowded corridor. The noise was coming nearer and growing louder. Jan turned his head and looked over his shoulder.

In the measured intervals between the piercing blasts of the whistle, the corridor was being illuminated by dazzling blue flashes. Although it was a long way off, Jan saw the cyborg immediately. It was head and shoulders taller than the people massed in front of it, and as the whistle shrieked, the warning beacon occluded and flashed from the blue light in its helmet. The St Bernard brain was functioning in perfect symbiosis with its homing systems as the cyborg headed towards the retrieval point with purposeful strides.

The crowds between Jan and the cyborg jostled frantically trying to get out of the way and flattening themselves against the walls of the corridor, like minnows scattering into the shallows and wriggling into weeds to escape from the rush of a pike. Some of them were striving, despite the increased pressure on all sides, to raise their hands to cover their ears.

The intervening crowd thinned out rapidly, and the cyborg was able to lengthen its stride and increase speed. The whistle began to hurt Jan's eardrums, and it was mixed with ultrasonics which made his head spin. The flashing light started to leave painful blotches of colour on the retinas of his eyes, so that he was forced to avert his gaze, and for the first time he looked down into the face of the unconscious man.

It was the face of a youth. The hair was thick and untidy, and it hung down over a wide white forehead which held worried wrinkles even in repose. The closed eyelids looked paper-thin and almost transparent, so that it was possible to imagine that the eyes could stare through them, even in sleep. There was a line of blood on the right cheek.

The crowd in the immediate vicinity had not completely dispersed, and Jan gently lowered the young man's shoulders onto the floor and stood back.

Now that he could see the face from a more natural angle, Jan decided that it was a face prematurely aged. It was the kind of face which acts as a page on which the sorrows of the world are written. And as he looked at that sorrowful face, watching it turn blue and white by turns, it seemed that it was in fact a blue face which turned white at each blast of the whistle, in accordance with the systole and diastole of some alien heart.

The eyes opened, searched the roof of the corridor, remembered, and turned sideways until they rested upon Jan's face.

'Don't worry,' Jan said. 'You are quite safe.'

The intermittent whistle blotted out every alternate word, and the unexpunged words appeared to be triggered by the blue flashes. Jan stood further

back, dizzy with the ultrasonics. This part of the
corridor was completely empty, apart from a line
of people pressed against the opposite wall. Jan
had never seen such a large area of floor-space in
the city, and the sight afflicted him with a sense of
unreality, as if part of the sea bed had suddenly
revealed itself.

The cyborg was only a few metres away, and it
covered the remaining distance in a few, rapid
strides. When it halted, and bent down to lift the
fallen man, there was an intermission in the whistl-
ing and the blue light locked on. The cyborg
straightened up, lifting the body on its forearms as
easily as if there was nothing there, and with its
first stride forward the whistle shrieked once
more.

The following crowd engulfed Jan Caspol, and
like a pent-up sea wave it carried him forward on
its crest. In front of the mob, but drawing away
with every stride, the cyborg whistled and flashed.
Jan continued to watch the tall figure until it moved
close to the wall, and disappeared with its burden
into a retrieval depot.

After it had gone, the massive crowd seemed to
be moving in perfect silence.

22

THE HUGE DOME of the Fun Palace modified the skyline. Nick Levantine was probably installed in there by now, or else in the Blue Star Club. The Fun Palace was the largest night club in the City, and offered the widest selection of aphrodollies, although some people preferred the greater intimacy of the Blue Star.

But Jan's thoughts were elsewhere as he drifted past on the slow lane of the northbound paveline. Now that he'd nothing else to think about, his mind was given over entirely to anguished reflections about Meriol.

Why? he asked himself. Why? Why had she left him without a word of explanation? Or rather, why had she sneaked away so that no word of explanation could be asked for?

He went over their meeting again, point by point, exercising total recall to capture every detail. It was like running a spool of film, and sometimes he delayed a frame, so that he could brood upon her face, or submit the smallest parts of the picture to analysis.

Meriol moved along the corridors of his memory with the power and vitality of an eidetic image. She returned to the round-topped table on which they'd left their drinks, and sat opposite him. Once again he watched the candle-light licking at her eyelids, her small freckled nose, and the lobes of her ears, and he saw the shadows playing around her mouth.

His memories were disrupted by the intrusion of the caged vacuum pump swallowing the moving paveline ahead of him, and he stepped off onto the sidewalk. He came out of the subway into the derelict compound, and the weed-strewn grass in that windless square was as still and silent as grass in a picture.

The click-clacking of his feet on the polished floor of the Gatehouse took Fred by surprise, and Jan caught him in the act of trying to hide a tall, uncorked bottle of Alsatian wine behind a Sèvres vase.

'G'evening, sir,' Fred said. 'I wasn't expecting you back this early, sir.'

Jan asked for a whisky, and sat in his favourite chair while Fred fluttered nervously about.

'All the Executives keeping well, sir?'

'I think so, Fred.'

Fred didn't seem to realize that his question was slightly out of place when put to someone who was returning from the city after an evening on his own.

'Naturally I never see most of them,' he flustered, as he brought the whisky. 'Never. And then there's one or two as I only see very occasional. Ve-ery occasional. There's a lady . . . er . . . '

'Val Steinberg?'

'No, sir. She still prefers her . . . ' Fred coughed

behind his hand. 'No, sir. I mean the lady who's a stahlex Executive.'

'Phillippa?' Jan said. 'Phillippa Mercer?'

'Yes, sir. Miss Mercer.' Fred picked up a duster, and flicked busily at one of the Sené chairs. 'I hope she's keeping well, sir?'

Jan couldn't stand Fred's prattling. He finished the whisky and stood up.

'So far as I know,' he said, as he moved towards the door with his right arm raised.

There were two autos in the parking ground besides his own. One was obviously Nick's, and he wasn't sure about the other. Fred was right. There weren't many visitors. There never had been.

Arnold Wilkins, for example, had visited the city only twice. The first time he was shocked by the total absence of birds. The second time he brought a basket of starlings, which he opened in the thruway, and the birds scrabbled about the windowless façades of the beeblocks until they were cleared out by the scavenger system.

Jan Caspol's disappointment twisted inside him all the way along the coast road.

Why? he asked himself again, as he looked at the white spume of the long waves, rolling noiselessly onto the pale sand. He stretched against the head rest like a man in pain.

He rolled his head. Far away on the left was the dark smudge of the conifer forest with the tall column of the fractionating tower growing out of it. He raised his eyes to Aldebaran, the red eye of the Bull, which winked and fluttered in the hot air above the Metals Plant.

Why? he asked. Why? After all, she'd actually come up to him at the bar. She'd made the first move. Jan reran the memory reels, with the irritable feeling that there was a clue somewhere.

The auto swung over into the slow lane and reduced speed in preparation for the left-hand turn. Jan sat forward and altered the co-ordinates. The auto gently accelerated and returned to the fast lane. An overwhelming sense of desolation made him unwilling to go home until he felt tired enough to fall asleep immediately.

The castellated outline of the Seaton Hotel appeared in the distance, and its lighted windows extended long fingers of welcome into the surrounding darkness. The auto slowed, and whispered through the gates to its parking spot.

Jan made his way through the dummy autos, and walked slowly up the steps. The robomanager came out to deliver his spiel, and Jan nodded an unconscious acknowledgement.

The chatter started the very moment he pushed the door to the lounge, filling the room with an illusion of camaraderie and fellow-feeling. Jan sat at the bar and punched himself a double measure of whisky.

Sipping his drink, he recalled the figure woven out of stahlex strip. That was another amazing thing. It wasn't anything like such a shattering experience as hearing Meriol sing, but it was another indication that the creative instinct was not completely dead, despite the Denaissance.

There was a gentle tap on his shoulder.

'Good evening, sir. Would you like to talk?'

Jan turned around, pondered for a second, and then smiled despite himself. 'Yes. I think I would.'

'I can talk about the influence of Zoroastrianism on the curried dishes of the Parsees, the Palladian—'

'No, no.' Jan said. 'I'd like somebody to talk to me about the Denaissance.'

'Certainly, sir. Any particular aspect?'

Jan considered. 'I'd like someone to talk about the reasons for the Denaissance.'

'Yes, sir. It will be our privilege, sir.'

The autopal turned smartly round, walked a few steps, then changed direction and proceeded to a table at the other end of the room. At the table heads were put together, and after a brief exchange another autopal got to his feet and came up to the bar.

'Good evening, sir. I believe you would like me to talk to you?'

'Yes,' Jan replied. 'I want to know what are considered to be the main factors which led up to the Denaissance.'

'Excuse me, sir. Do you mean you would like me to review the literature and art of the Pre-Denaissance Period?'

'No,' Jan said. 'Not unless it's necessary to do so. I just want to know why people became incapable of creating literature, or any other kind of art.'

'I understand, sir. I shall give you the benefit of the most recent thinking about the subject.'

There was a slight pause as a hidden retrieval mechanism located the required portion of the talks bank. When the autopal spoke again it was with a new voice which used the clean gutturals and pure vowels of the North East coast, touched with a slight American twang.

It had been the accent of the intellectual élite for almost a century.

23

'IT USED TO BE THOUGHT', said the new voice, 'that the death of the creative instinct in modern times was due to relatively recent changes in the environment. It was argued, for example, that genetic engineering and postnatal amplification had produced an Executive class in which very high intelligence had been achieved at the expense of destroying the creative faculties. It was argued, similarly, that the Citizens were incapable of achieving anything because of their conditioning. However, these views are now considered too naïve, and the reasons for the disappearance of contemporary literature and the other arts are further to seek.'

Jan sipped his whisky and listened attentively. It was one way of killing time, and besides, he might gain some insight into Meriol's personality.

'To find the answer you have to go back to the development of the steam engine. Savery built his pumping engine, and Newcomen improved upon it. Although that was the beginning of modern technology, these early engines made little difference to the general condition of life. But things really started to change with the arrival of James Watt, and the rotary motion of his engine released industry from the water-wheel and therefore from the banks of rivers. The steam engine then became not only the spearhead of technological advance, but also the basis of large scale organization and the development of managerial skills. And it was a Watt engine which George Stephenson was to examine when—'

Jan interrupted. 'Wait a minute. What's this got to do with my question? It strikes me I'm listening to the wrong programme.'

'Not at all, sir.' The autopal overrode the recording in suave tones. 'If you continue to listen I am sure you will find your question answered satisfactorily.'

The northern voice continued. 'Before the development of steam power you'd always had millwrights, blacksmiths, carpenters, potters, weavers, masons, and so on. Their activities were part of a way of life. The kind of work they did was transferred quite spontaneously and unselfconsciously into literature, and even into poetry. Shakespeare, for example, thought naturally in their terms, and his plays abound with references to the technologies of his day.

'I shall illustrate what I mean by a few quotations from Shakespeare, beginning with references to the various operations of carpentry.

'Let's start with dovetailing:

> *this fellow will but join you together as they join wainscott; then one of you will prove a shrunk panel, and like green timber warp, warp.*
>
> As You Like It, Act 3 Scene 3.

'Now let's have a few examples from coopering:

Grapple them to thy soul with hoops of steel
Hamlet, Act 1 Scene 3.

Confirm'd, confirm'd! O, that is stronger made
Which was before barr'd up with ribs of iron!
Much Ado About Nothing, Act 4 Scene 1.

'Now for a few examples concerned with nails, screws, and rivets—'

'All right,' Jan intercepted. 'You've made your point. You can skip the other quotations.'

The retrieval device traversed, and then the voice recommenced. 'But steam power introduced a new kind of man. This was the engineer. The techniques of the engineer were not assimilated in the same way as those of the earliest craftsmen had been, and this was due to a failure of empathy.'

The autopal paused, as if to emphasize that what followed was of particular importance.

'This failure in empathy was the source of the trouble. Perhaps, you see, James Watt was hammering, chipping, and filing away at his primitive engines with all the passionate frenzy of Michelangelo hewing his Moses out of Carrara marble. But nobody knew and nobody cared. Nobody made an act of imaginative sympathy which would have brought the steam engine into the main stream of thought and feeling. This divergence led to the exclusion of the engineer and all his works from the subjects considered worthy of treatment by an artist.'

Jan sipped his whisky and nodded.

'The situation was made worse by the provincialism of the old capital and the south. As always, the people of London couldn't believe that anything important was happening outside their city boundaries. And to the superficially educated gentry of what used to be called the Home Counties, the development of railways in the north was no more than a threat to fox hunting and grouse coverts. But I know what you're thinking. You're thinking I've forgotten that clockwork preceded steam as a motive power.'

Jan Caspol jumped. He hadn't been thinking anything of the kind.

'I admit that Huygens predated the engineers, and you could have seen trains of gears and crown wheels in clocks well before the development of the steam engine. But the early clocks were rare and expensive. Most people didn't see them, and when they did the machinery was often hidden in cases. By the time clocks became commonplace it was steam technology, and not clockwork, which had fixed the status of engineering.'

Jan punched himself another large whisky. He couldn't see this argument telling him much about Meriol.

'The failure in empathy is more extraordinary the more you think about it. The building of railways in England was the most gargantuan enterprise undertaken by mankind since the building of the pyramids. As if by divine ordinance England produced, at exactly the same time, its greatest crop of poets of genius. But what did the poets write about? Wordsworth wrote about daffodils, Coleridge about Kubla Khan, Byron about ancient Rome, Shelley about skylarks, and Keats about Grecian urns.'

It was a juxtaposition Jan had never made.

'All this mightn't have mattered so much', resumed the autopal, 'if the poets of the early 19th century hadn't been so indisputably great. As it was, their simultaneous impact was overwhelming, and they shaped the literary tradition for over a century. One of the most stupendous sights of Victorian England must have been to see a Daniel Gooch engine running up and down to Paddington on Brunel's railway. But where was the poet laureate?'

Jan shrugged.

'Tennyson was sitting on his lordly arse in a hostelry at Caerleon, writing about Queen Guinevere and the Knights of the Round Table.'

But what about the paintings of Turner, Jan reflected, and then smiled at a private thought. Perhaps the analogy between piston engines and sex made the early products of the machine age particularly abhorrent to the Victorians.

'So literature conspired to perpetuate a confidence trick, a monstrous sleight-of-hand, by which the new world of the engineer was excluded from that part of experience which was called culture. People quoted Byron and Shelley, who made the mountains beautiful, but ignored Abt and Riggenbach, who made them accessible. When a poet did try to describe the new world, he couldn't find an appropriate language. Listen to this sonnet, which is entitled The Arriving Train.

> *Behold, smoke panoplied, the wondrous car,*
> *Strong and impetuous, but obedient still;*
> *Behold it comes–'*

Jan interrupted. 'Please miss out the rest of it.'

'A jingling of once bright coins', said the autopal, 'worn thin and dull by the fingers of innumerable poets who—'

'And miss out your reflections upon it,' Jan said.

The retrieval mechanism traversed. 'It seemed for a time as if the situation might be different in architecture, where iron was used by Brunel, Robert Stephenson, Telf—'

'Skip it,' said Jan. 'It's all in the text books.'

'Dickens's hatred of the steam engine, and his caricatures of businessmen, did a great deal of harm by—'

'Skip that as well.'

'A few drops of economic reality splashed into the Edwardian novel, but in the 1920s there—'

'Please move on a bit.' Jan would have sounded irritable if he hadn't been so tired. 'This is all old stuff.'

The autopal obeyed. 'And so a situation grew up in which the writer became completely divorced from, and usually hostile to, the workings of the economic system. Thomas Mann in his insurance office, Priestley in his textile office, Kafka in his—

Jan yawned, and looked at his chrono. 'Can you go on to the conclusion?'

After a pause the voice continued. 'And so, ultimately, by the time of the Pre-Denaissance Period, all the people of great general ability were in business corporations of one kind or another. On the other hand, the writers and artists were people who were incapable of executive responsibility, and they could use their narrow aptitudes to describe only a dwindling area of experience which was of little interest to the most intelligent part of the population. An interface had been finally erected between art and technology which nobody wanted to cross. When computer-generated art and literature started to fill the vacuum the Denaissance Period began, and since that time . . . '

The autopal's sensors indicated that the listener had fallen asleep, sitting upright at the bar with his chin in his hand. The voice became silent, but the autopal remained standing near enough to give assistance if the sleeper showed any signs of falling from his seat.

Jan Caspol was dreaming. He and Meriol were joined together like the component parts of a precision-made high-pressure steam engine. They were moving with the complex balance and oiled rhythm of Walschaerts valve gear. After each thrust of the piston against the stuffing box the spent vapours were exhausted through the funnel of her mouth in sharp, stabbing sobs.

He awoke with a start, and looked round the silent room. All those photoelectric eyes clicked open with one accord, and the chatter around the tables recommenced.

The chatter didn't cease until the door had closed behind him.

24

JAN CASPOL SAT in the swivel chair in his systems lounge, and his hand hovered over the console before he selected a stud and punched the order. A tapered glass containing warm milk whipped into a froth with two raw eggs and a dash of whisky coasted into his waiting hand.

'All right,' he said to the voiceprint analyzer, and swivelled round to face the display screen. 'Any messages?'

The white lettering appeared.

> *mr. bendix of north eastern stockholders corp. has sent hand-written note thanking you for entertaining him yesterday & saying how much he enjoyed tour of the works. text runs to 227 words & does not call for specific comment. do you wish to view it?*

Jan sipped his drink. 'No. Get out a standard reply and put it through the cliché scrambler, but match the greeting and valediction. Transpose into my handwriting and send it off. Anything else?'

yes. from mr tilling of aerospace corp. as
follows: did you watch götterdämmerung &
did you enjoy it?
> *bruder-brunstig*
> *mutig gemischt*
> *blüh' im trank unser blut!*

Jan smiled wanly. 'Tell him the answer is *yes* on
both counts. And add *treue trink' ich dem freund!*
Anything else?'

no other messages

He asked for the news bulletin, and as it unrolled
he scanned it with his usual concentration. The
Japanese robot team on Mars had uncovered iron
ore in Tharsis with a rumoured Fe content of over
90%. Jan stopped the bulletin and asked for a note
on the richest historical earth ores.

The screen blanked and presented on the right a
stationary world outline map with numbered loca-
tions, while on the left a scrupulously detailed
statistical key began to uproll.

'Condense it!' Jan shouted. 'All I want is a short
narrative.'

The screen blanked again.

> *hematite fe$_2$o$_3$) up to 68% fe at itabira &*
> *samitri (brazil) yampi sound & mt.*
> *goldsworthy (australia) marcona (peru).*
> *magnetite (fe$_3$o$_4$) up to 65% fe at kiruna &*
> *gallivare (sweden) magnitogorsk . . .*

Jan filed the data away in his short term memory. It was precisely the kind of information which
Steinberg expected people to carry about with
them.

The news bulletin resumed its upward course, and Jan's eyes followed a middle line through the hurrying text. As he expected, a tremendous row was brewing over Queen Elizabeth III's pregnancy. There were those who said it would be absurd if the future sovereign were the only individual outside city walls with only average intelligence or worse. Those who opposed them maintained that chromosomal adjustments to the royal foetus would infringe the hereditary principle.

'Good,' Jan said, yawning and stretching his legs. 'Let's have a look at the orders. Any divergences from forecast?'

He began to raise the drink to his mouth, but stopped before the glass was halfway there. At first he thought there'd been a malfunction in the system. The background to the display screen had changed, faster than the flutter of an eyelid, from black to brilliant white; and for the first time ever the lettering was an electroluminous red.

> *yes. there is significant divergence from forecast. do you want details?*

Jan placed his glass on top of the control desk with an unsteady hand and started to smile. His amusement was silent at first, but then it welled up inside him, hurting his stomach, until he laughed out loud. It had happened! It had finally happened! He could hardly believe it.

He collected himself, and a puckish spirit forced the next words out of his mouth.

'No,' he said in a strangled voice. 'No details today, but thanks all the same.'

He choked with laughter on the last word, and lay back helpless in his swivel chair. Through streaming eyes he saw that the screen remained a brilliant white and the lettering a startling red, but the text had changed.

> *strongly recommend you request details. there is significant divergence from forecast. repeat. there is significant divergence from forecast.*

Jan's hilarity slowly subsided, and he wiped his eyes. The spirit of mischief disappeared as mysteriously as it had come, and all his faculties were directed to the job in hand when he spoke again.

'All right. Let's see the details.'

The display screen reverted to its usual dark background and white lettering, and projected the statistical table for Consumers. Everything was normal, and the largest divergence expressed in terms of standard deviation from expected trend was only ·09.

'Fade,' he said.

The screen winked and presented the statistical table for Stockholders. The background was still black with white text, except for a brilliant white band under everything relating to North Eastern Stockholders on which the lettering was an electroluminous red.

The statistics showed that North Eastern Stockholders Corporation had ordered a fantastic tonnage during the previous twenty-four hours, far in excess of historical levels and the extrapolated forecast, which threw up a positive divergence in the final column of 2·30.

The foveae centralis of Jan's eyes scanned the data from left to right, picking up every digit from the table and imprinting it in his memory circuits.

'Fade.'

He drained his glass, shoved it into the return chute, and thumbed the whisky button.

'Show me North Eastern Stockholders' order pattern on an annual basis,' he commanded.

The display screen presented another table data. In the left-hand column was a list of the different items purchased: sheets, blocks, strip, fibres, and a variety of shapes with their dimensions and specifications. Reading from left to right were the annual tonnages ordered against each item for the previous twelve years.

'Now show me the order pattern on a monthly basis,' he instructed.

The screen blinked and substituted monthly tonnages for the previous twelve months against each item.

'Now show it on a weekly basis.'

The screen blinked again and substituted weekly tonnages against each item for the previous three months.

'Now daily.'

The screen projected the required data for the previous two weeks, and Jan added this to the accumulating mass of information in his memory circuits.

'Fade,' he said.

Jan swallowed some whisky, and wrinkled his brow. Lighting a felicity, he issued another command.

'Let me see the activity indices.'

The screen showed a list of the major industries which consumed stahlex, but at that moment the video buzzed and the big display screen blanked automatically.

'What the bloody hell's going on?' Nick Levantine's voice was yelling into the room before his face was fully defined on the video.

Jan turned to view the small screen. 'Don't get so excited.'

'Don't get so excited!' There were sparks of anger in Nick's dark eyes. 'I come in this morning and find that the spare sphere has been on stream since midnight because some maniac has ordered sufficient stahlex to plug half the craters on the moon.'

Jan smiled. 'I thought you were going to congratulate me on my salesmanship.'

'Don't be ridiculous!' Nick wasn't amused. 'You know as well as I do that it shouldn't happen. Damn it all, Jan, the plant is now working at absolute capacity, and I'm still waiting for confirmation that we're operating within the safety parameters of heat-sinking. If this keeps up we won't be able to accommodate so much as an upward wobble in the order intake. Do you understand?'

Jan spoke more seriously. 'Of course I do. I was in the middle of my investigations when you so rudely interrupted. So if you don't mind . . . '

Jan moved his hand to disconnect.

'Have you told Steinberg yet?' Nick asked.

'No,' said Jan. 'And I've got quite a bit of work to do before I tell him.'

Nick's features relaxed into a wide grin, and he raised a half empty glass of Newcastle Brown Ale. 'And the best of luck,' he said.

25

NICK LEVANTINE CLEARED the display screen of the previous twenty-four hours production data, put his feet on the control console, and relaxed. There was nothing else for him to do until he received confirmation that they were still operating within the required heat-sinking parameters.

Lighting a felicity, he blew mauve smoke towards the spirographs which decorated the main wall of his systems lounge, and reached for the half-finished glass of Newcastle Brown Ale. He was looking forward to this evening.

Linda was everything he'd ever asked for in a woman. So far as he was concerned, she was the perfect aphrodolly. Nick swallowed some ale, and recalled their encounter three nights ago. There was only one thing wrong with her. She'd made him wait until tonight before he saw her again. If it hadn't been for that, his experience of last night wouldn't have happened.

Nick tried to give himself up to thoughts of Linda, remembering what she had been like three nights ago and anticipating what she would be like tonight, but thoughts of last night flooded his memory tracks.

He was in his usual place at the Fun Palace, and

as he lowered his opera glasses he saw an aphrodolly drifting up towards him. His attention was caught immediately when she stepped off the escalator into the row of seats where he was stationed.

She presented the gestalt of a grande dame. The hair was dressed in a tall pompadour, greyed with powder, and pomaded in ringlets. A spray of violet plumes was set upright on her head, and there was a bow of black velvet at the back. Half her face was covered with a black mask, and a black beauty patch adorned one cheek.

Nick was intrigued.

He could see the points of pearl grey satin shoes, peeping from beneath a violet under-skirt festooned with black net. Nick's demon took over, and he moved along to sit beside her. She turned to face him.

The neckline of her pearl-grey gown was high at the back, but low at the front. There was a black velvet ribbon round her neck, beneath which his eyes caressed the incipient swelling of her breasts. She looked as if she'd stepped out of a comedy by Marivaux, and was now on her way to some secret assignment at a *fête d'amour*.

Nick bent to make his request.

'*Si, señor,*' she murmured.

He supported her bare arm, beneath the ruched sleeve, to help her onto the escalator. But she snatched her arm away, and maintained her aristocratic hauteur, even when they were crushed together on the paveline.

As they crammed into the elevator chamber she knocked his hands away. He resigned himself to the fact that this pretence at circumspection was all part of the gestalt, and was supposed to lend an added piquancy to the situation. The aphrodolly provided the persona and the environment, and the lover assumed the rôle which best suited his basic cravings for dominance or submission.

He was the favoured lackey of an Italian Countess, or her *cavaliere servente* and *cicisbeo*, another Byron to another La Guiccioli; or he was the gamekeeper and donkey boy of so many fictions and *journals intimes*; or one of the Empress Catherine's humble lovers, Zoritch or Lanskoy.

She kept him at arm's length in the module. With growing impatience he crawled into the aphrocell, and she followed. She wanted to keep the light off, but he insisted it be turned on.

The scenario represented a large room in a Venetian plazzo. Dancing lights from a Murano chandelier were reflected in cheval mirrors, and the window was open to the warm night air. Outside, the waters of the canal lapped gently at the ancient stonework of a city which was now submerged.

Nick raised his hand to remove the black mask, but she restrained him with her jewelled fingers. With a shrug he turned his attention elsewhere.

He pulled at the front of her gown, and her white breasts appeared over its grey horizon like the two moons of Mars. She had the small, high breasts of a Van Eyck Virgin, and the nipples were crowned with gold discs like the heads of Byzantine saints.

Nick's fingers, as skilful and quick as a surgeon's, found their way through a silk chemise and a quilted petticoat, discovered a corset stiffened with stahlex rods, and got to work on a multiplicity of tapes and buttons. She trembled under his connoisseur's hands.

Her patrician dignity began to ebb away under his touch. As he unrolled the pearl-grey stockings she went to pieces and arched towards him. Nick raised his hand to rip off the black mask.

The video buzzed. He turned towards it and saw Phillippa's face, white and drawn, with puffy swellings under the eyes as blue as bruises.

'I'm just confirming that we're operating within the heat-sinking parameters,' she said.

'All right.'

'There's only a small safety margin, but we're inside.'

He reached out to disconnect.

'Nick.'

'Yes?'

'There's one other thing.'

'What?'

Phillippa hesitated, and her bottom lip thinned and widened as she nipped it between her teeth. 'Nick. About last night. I—'

'Forget it,' he said, savagely.

'But, Nick, I want you to understand that I went to all that trouble only because I—'

Nick reached out again, and this time he did disconnect.

26

'LET ME SEE the activity indices,' repeated Jan.

Once again the display screen presented a list of the major industries which consumed stahlex with coefficients of their stahlex-intensity. Next to each industrial category there was a series of index numbers, historical, current, and projected, based on year 2100=100.

Jan asked for these industrial categories to be broken down into their component parts. This meant, for example, that *Civil Engineering* was split up into its different sectors such as City Beeblocks, Executive Houses, Pavelines, Autoways, Bridges, Spaceports, and Power Stations. A matching array of indices showed the pattern of demand for stahlex from these different sectors.

After that he asked to see all the activity indices broken down on a regional basis, so as to determine whether there was any reason why the demand for stahlex in the North East should have moved against the national trend.

As his eyes scanned the figures he dropped his felicity into the atomizer, and automatically lit another one. He swallowed some more whisky.

'Economic indicators, please.'

The display screen presented another table of

index numbers, again based on year 2100=100, showing trends in Population Growth, Consumer Spending, Executive Credits, Aphrocollege Graduations, Fertilizers, Aerospace Research, Paveline Maintenance, and the Venusian and Martian Mining Projects. Once more he asked for a breakdown on a regional basis.

'Fade,' he said despondently.

Jan sat back in his swivel chair, inhaled deeply, and blew mauve smoke in the direction of the display screen. Throwing his head back he swallowed the remains of his whisky, pushed his empty glass into the return chute, and turned to the video.

'Get me Mr Bendix of North Eastern Stockholders.'

The screen lightened, and Bendix stared back at him with bulging eyes.

'Hello, David.' Jan was all smiles. 'Thanks for the note. No need to ask whether you got home all right.'

They swapped a few inanities about the pleasures of the day before.

'I thought I'd give you a call,' Jan continued, 'regarding the lift in your orders.'

'Didn't I mention that I might have to make an adjustment?'

'Yes.' Jan found it difficult to maintain his smile at full exposure. 'But it never crossed my mind that you meant an adjustment of this magnitude.'

Bendix reflected the smile. 'I assume you can cope with the extra tonnage?'

'Oh certainly. Certainly.' Jan waved his arm to dismiss the possibility of any other answer. 'We can cope all right. There's no worry about that. However . . .'

'Yes?'

'Just as a matter of academic interest, I couldn't help wondering what had induced such a heavy increase in your order rate.'

'It's quite simple,' Bendix said. 'When I took over control of North Eastern Stockholders I discovered that they've been selling fractionally more than they've been buying, right across the range, for a long time. It's only a tiny discrepancy, but it wasn't registered by the control systems, and nobody had actually looked in the warehouse for ages. So although the discrepancy was very small, the cumulative effect over a long period has been considerable. In fact when I instituted a physical inventory I discovered the warehouse was virtually empty.'

Jan tried to keep the feeling of relief out of his voice. 'So it's a one-off operation to put your stock levels right.'

'Exactly.' Bendix nodded.

'In other words,' said Jan, determined to be absolutely clear about the matter, 'we can't look forward to repeat orders of the same size.'

'Bendix smiled. 'I'm afraid not, Jan. I can assure you that we'll never burden you with such large orders again.'

Bendix's smile grew into a laugh in which Jan forced himself to join.

'By the way,' Jan added. 'Presumably your future order rate will be slightly higher than it was previously, to compensate for the previous error?'

'You're quite right, Jan. But so little higher you'll not notice it.'

'*Hardly* notice it,' Jan corrected.

'Very well. You'll *hardly* notice it. I haven't determined how much more it'll be, but I can tell you it will be very small.'

'All the same,' Jan persisted. 'I'd be grateful if you'd let me know the revised figures as soon as you can. Then I can pass them on to Arnold Wilkins, our Comptroller, so that he can update his DSM models.'

Bendix promised every co-operation, and his face faded from the screen. Jan reflected that when the Cheshire cat disappeared it was the smile which remained. With Bendix, it was the eyes which were the last feature to vanish.

Jan proceeded with the most unpleasant part of the day's work.

27

STEINBERG'S HEAD, AS ALWAYS, appeared to be several sizes too large for the video screen. 'You're late this morning, Caspol.'

'Yes, sir.'

'Why?'

'It couldn't be helped, sir. I wanted to do a little investigation before I contacted you.'

'Why?'

Jan Caspol decided, not without some small degree of relish, to dispense with a prologue. 'There's a positive divergence of 2·3 sigma against a customer forecast.'

'What!'

Steinberg's head seemed to swell and distort in the screen, like a balloon being inflated in a bottle. The hairless ridges above his eyes pushed up against the mountainous brow, creating a moulded contour map which threw the fjords and crevasses into shadowed relief. His face turned as grey as a slug's belly, and then a spot of pink appeared in each cheek, as startling and unexpected as tea roses on the polar caps.

Jan waited, slightly alarmed by the effects of his revelation.

The arteries in Steinberg's head distended to accommodate his racing blood. The pink spots in his cheeks went out like lights, and his grey skin looked wet.

'Give me the details,' he said, and his voice sounded thin despite the amplifier and tone control.

Jan did.

'I see,' said Steinberg. 'North Eastern Stockholders. And you entertained Bendix yesterday?'

'Yes, sir.'

'Did he say there was a possibility of such an increase in his orders?'

'He said he might adjust, but there was no hint of such a—'

'Isn't it curious that Bendix should step up his orders immediately after being shown round the works by the GK Series 7B?'

'I don't think so, sir. I think the extra tonnage and the tour of the works are both effects of the same cause.'

Steinberg's brow crinkled again. 'Don't talk to me in that metaphysical manner.'

'I'm sorry, sir. I meant to say that the extra tonnage and the tour of the works both arise from the fact that Bendix is the new broom at North Eastern Stockholders Corporation.'

'Hmm.' Steinberg appeared doubtful. 'And you say that this sudden increase in demand isn't related to any of the demand parameters?'

'No, sir. The point is that—'

'This sudden increase in demand cannot be correlated with any movement in any of the Activity Indices or Economic Indicators, no matter how they are analyzed?'

'No, sir.'

'You were going to make a point, I believe.'

'Yes,' said Jan. 'The increase in demand is not really sudden. It's simply that we're experiencing the results of a very small under-estimate of demand in one region, which has been accumulating for a long time, and which—'

Jan noticed that veins as fat as worms were crawling across the amplified temporal lobes above Steinberg's ears. The knotted veins pulsed and pumped as they struggled to feed the ganglia, which lay visible under the stretched flesh of the skull, like starfishes from which the nerve fibres irradiated with the stiff expectancy of fingers on an open hand.

'Did you want to speak, sir?' asked Jan.

'I thought I might,' Steinberg said. His fury had increased his vocal frequency to a degree where the tone control became partially ineffective and the words issued forth in a hiss. 'I was trying to bring you to the point where you would admit that your sales estimates have been wrong. Wrong by a small amount, I agree. But wrong. And wrong for a long time, as you say.'

'Yes, sir.'

'Computer-to-computer order systems don't work particularly well in this industry when there are lunatics in control. And I want to know what you're going to do about it.'

Jan tried to choose his words carefully. 'We shall clear the extra tonnage within this twenty-four hour cycle, and then revert to equilibrium working. Bendix has promised me his revised estimates. These will be very little higher than the previous estimates, but I shall pass them to Mr

Wilkins so that he can—'

'What about the Activity Indices?' asked Steinberg.

'I'll probably adjust the index for Miscellaneous End Uses.'

Steinberg's face darkened. 'I detest residual figures and balancing items.'

'As I've just said, sir, the revised estimates will be very little higher than—'

Steinberg's face darkened to a deeper shade, and the corded veins above his ears were an oily blue. 'And as I've just said, I don't like residual figures and balancing items. Doesn't this fool Bendix know where the extra tonnage is going?'

'No, sir. It's simply that because of previous errors—'

'Shut up,' said Steinberg. 'I don't want to listen to that rubbish again. Have *you* any idea where additional stahlex might be going?'

'Well . . .'

'Get on with it, Caspol.'

'Well, sir,' Jan said, regretting his words almost as he said them. 'I did see a kind of ornamental figure in the city made out of fine gauge stahlex strip. If that sort of thing became a craze we might find—'

'What!' Steinberg's mouth dropped open, and he peered out of the video screen like a giant cod fish in an aquarium. 'You mean some sort of contemporary art work?'

'Yes, sir.'

'Where was this? In a hairdressing shop, or somewhere like that?'

'Yes, sir.'

Jan felt inclined to smile for the first time since Steinberg's head appeared on the video. It was one of Steinberg's blind spots that he refused to believe that there could be any reason for visiting the city other than to get one's hair cut. Perhaps the blind spot developed out of an inability to accept the facts of his daughter's way of life.

Steinberg's astonishment disappeared, and was replaced by another show of temper. 'But this kind of activity, although completely unexpected, affects only the demand for stahlex strip.'

'Admittedly.' Jan wished he hadn't mentioned it. 'And then only to an insignificant degree.'

Steinberg pondered in silence, and Jan watched his graven face.

Steinberg must have read every line of poetry which had ever been printed, heard every bar of music which had ever been composed, seen every painting, sculpture, and building which was worth viewing. It was impossible that he should ever again climb some unknown mountain of the spirit, only to discover some higher peak on the other side, with its summit lost in clouds of mystery and delight.

Not for the first time, Jan experienced a feeling of pity for Steinberg.

The criss-cross avenues of Kulturgesichte must be as familiar to him as the foot-paths in his own garden, and the unfailing memory made it impossible for there to be any element of re-discovery or suprise. For Steinberg the pleasures of the intellect must be as dead as those of the body.

'Caspol.'

'Yes, sir.'

'Tell Levantine and Wilkins that I want a joint report on the technical and economic implications of operating above the equilibrium level by 1800 today. Tell Mercer that I want an immediate assurance regarding heat-sinking. Tell that idiot Peters that I don't want any of his nonsense. No publicity at all. Peters will probably think that this is an ideal opportunity to tell the world that we're breaking all production records, whereas all this wretched affair proves is that our Sales Executive is utterly incapable of assessing the demand for our products.'

The screen blanked.

Jan lit a felicity, and put in the first call.

'It seems a bit hard,' Nick complained. 'The sales department get the order book in such a terrible tangle that the production department have to spend the afternoon sorting it all out.'

Jan smiled. 'A bit of overtime will do you good.'

'I can't face Wilkie before I've had some fresh air,' said Nick. 'What about splashing our pipes in the Seaton Hotel?'

28

NICK LEVANTINE PUNCHED two pints of Newcastle Brown Ale and handed one of them across.

'So that's why I saw your auto parked outside the Gatehouse,' he said. 'Yesterday must be the first time you've beaten me into the city.'

Jan nodded. 'And today will be the second.'

'By a good margin, too', Nick grimaced, 'but there's no need to rub it in. Steinberg contacted me just as I was about to leave. Besides preparing that joint report with Wilkie this afternoon, he wants me to collect Henry's records.'

'Why?' Jan wasn't really interested.

'So that he can play back the questions your customer asked him, I suppose.'

Jan's thoughts were elsewhere. 'I don't know whether going to the Fiesta Club so early will do any good. If I have no more success than last night it'll be a waste of time.'

'Don't underestimate the experience.' Nick spluttered into his ale in anticipation of the joke. 'I'll bet you had some pleasant dreams about her organ.'

Jan winced.

'But perhaps I've got it all wrong,' Nick persisted. 'Although this organ of hers is so old-fashioned, I suppose it's equipped with the usual electronic gadgetry?'

'I suppose so.'

'And she plays and sings, and you've never heard either the music or the songs before?'

'That's one of the extraordinary things about her,' Jan said.

'On the contrary,' said Nick. 'It's the *only* extraordinary thing about her.' He crashed his glass on the bar to add emphasis to his conclusion. 'You've merely been bowled over by a genuine example of psychoelectronic symbiosis. A shattering of the interface.'

Jan shook his head and smiled. 'I wish that's all it was.'

'Look here, Jan. I can't have this nonsense. You're suffering from an illusory disease, and its imaginary ravages can be cured by the application of reason. Or, if reason isn't sufficient, by the regular and conscientious application of aphrodollies. You've been infected by the fictitious virus invented by a sickly troubadour, or Chrestien de Troyes, or some other courtly French bum.'

'Phillippa wouldn't agree with you. She thinks it was invented earlier, in Doric Sicily.'

At the mention of Phillippa, Nick's face clouded. 'Don't mention that woman to me.'

'Why do you say that?' asked Jan, remembering Phillippa's woes despite his own. 'When I spoke to her on the video this morning I thought she looked quite attractive.'

'Phillipa!'

'Yes. I think the way her hair—'

Nick's striking face was made ugly by his loathing. 'I detest the woman. She completely fulfils the saint's definition of woman as a bag of excrement. If you asked me to describe the most horrible death imaginable, I'd say it would be to expire with that insufferable woman's arms round my neck.'

Jan was taken unawares by the strength of Nick's hatred. In the ensuing silence the subdued chatter of the autopals became audible, and the soft strains of Raphael Rozier wafted on the air.

'Anyway,' Nick said, determined to change the subject. 'If you want to see me this evening I'll be in the Blue Star. I've an appointment there that I wouldn't miss for anything.'

Jan smiled. Even Leporello couldn't have listed all Nick's women.

Nick swallowed, and slid his empty glass across the bar. 'I'd better be getting back to contact Wilkie and start this joint report. Think about me while you're having a gay time in the city.'

'I'll try to.' Jan finished his drink.

Nick led the way out of the bar, and down the stone steps of the Seaton Hotel.

'And don't forget what I told you', he called, as they parted company in the parking ground, 'about that old-fashioned cure for your virus.'

Jan's auto swung out onto the coast road and moved into the fast lane. The broadsweep of the golden sands was on the left. It was those limitless reserves of silica which had determined the Americans to locate the British stahlex works on the North East coast, and it seemed incredible that those desert soils were being continuously siphoned away by the underground chutes.

On the right the red deer raised their heads as the auto passed. Behind them the coniferous forest screened the stahlex works, as uninhabited as a

forsaken city, and out of the dark green foliage the
southbound monorail ran as straight as an arrow to
pierce the wall of the Second Sector.

The auto breathed into its appointed parking
spot, Jan slid out, raised his right arm, and entered
the Gatehouse.

'G'evening. I mean g'afternoon, sir.'

Jan thought Fred would have been more surprised to see him, partly because he was becoming
such a regular visitor, and partly because he had
arrived so early. But Fred appeared to have other
things on his mind, or else he'd washed his lunch
down with rather too much Alsatian wine.

'The usual, sir?'

'Thank you, Fred.'

Jan equipped himself with a whisky flask and a
supply of money, and turned towards the door.

'There's just one thing, Mr Caspol.'

Jan paused in the act of raising his left arm.
'What's that?'

'Well, sir.' Fred coughed behind his hand. 'It's
just that I 'appened to look out some time ago and I
seen someone 'anging about.'

Jan's arm dropped to his side. 'What! In the
compound?'

'Exactly, sir. In the compound as you say. A bit
suspicious looking. At least', Fred shuffled his feet
and corrected himself, 'what some folk might call
sort of suspicious looking. I know that sort of thing
is supposed to be impossible, sir, but I thought I'd
mention it.'

'Thank you, Fred. I'll keep my eyes open.'

'Thank you, sir.'

Jan raised his left arm again, and the receptors in
the door jamb identified the sintered cobalt hierog-
lyph embedded in the radial bone.

The compound was deserted as always. But when he left the faded, yellow grass behind and turned into the thruway, there was a shabby figure on the widewalk having difficulty in lighting a felicity.

It was the first time Jan had ever seen anyone in the vicinity of the terminus or the vacuum pump.

29

JAN CASPOL TRAVELLED in the fast lane of the southbound paveline as far as the Fun Palace, then crossed to the other side by the subway. In Vulcan Road the tiny alleyways ran right and left, each one named after a defunct metal. He plunged into the dark tunnel and shouldered his way through the crowds pressing into the Anvil Bar.

The illuminated sign of the Fiesta Club glowed in the blackness of Tubal Lane. He pushed at the unpainted door and mounted the creaking stairs.

In the brightly lit ante-room the man with the Sicilian moustache looked as if he was about to make some reference to the previous evening, but Jan put his money on the table and went straight through into the club. He sat at the nearest table and looked around the shadowy room.

Despite the early hour there were a few people already present. A man and a woman in a close embrace. A couple of drunken youths. And at a table in the deepest shadows, next to the red velvet curtain, two girls with heads close together.

He jerked to his feet and crossed the room.

'Meriol?' he said.

She didn't turn her head. But the girl with whom she was sitting looked up into his face and smiled. The girl's beauty was striking, and she exuded sensuality like a perfume.

'Meriol!' he repeated.

She turned her head slightly. 'Go away.'

'But, Meriol! Why?'

He snatched a chair from the next table and sat down opposite the two girls. Meriol's eyelids were lowered and her hands were out of sight.

'Meriol,' he begged. 'Don't you remember me? I'm Jan Caspol.'

She didn't move, nor acknowledge by so much as the trembling of an eyelid that she'd heard him. The other girl, however, showed added interest and looked at him appraisingly.

Jan's eyes were drawn to the other girl for a moment. She was almost certainly an aphrodolly. Rich, auburn curls clustered round her head, and her lips were full. When she smiled her canines were prominent, which according to Lavater's old physiognomical rules was a sure sign of lust in women. Jan couldn't help registering the fact that she was a woman with all the specific gestalt criteria that Nick Levantine most coveted.

But he promptly returned his attention to Meriol.

'Don't you remember me?' he persisted. 'I came here two nights ago and heard you sing and I came last night and I thought we . . . I didn't mind you going away although I was disappointed. But you can't have forgotten. You remember, don't you. We had a drink together and I thought we . . . '

Meriol's eyelids lifted, and when the multi-coloured eyes looked into his he projected upon them a spasm of mixed emotions: searching, finding, losing; love, hate, anger.

Jan reached over the table to seize her elbow. She pulled her arm away, and he sensed the movement of her hand under the table as it sought and found the responding clasp of her companion. Meriol stood up and the girl stood up with her. They were still holding hands.

'Don't go,' he pleaded.

Meriol began to walk past him, half pulling the other girl behind her, but Jan leaped up and blocked their way.

'Listen,' he said, desperately. 'Please listen to me.'

She looked briefly into his face and then looked down. 'No,' she said, softly. 'I don't want to listen and I don't want to see you. I don't want to see you ever again and I never shall.'

'But, Meriol . . . '

He was tempted to grab her by the arms. But she stepped sideways and brushed past him, holding tightly onto her friend's hand. With her free hand she knocked the red curtain aside, opened the door, and both girls disappeared into the dressing room.

Jan became aware of heads turned in his direction, and one of the drunken youths laughing. He didn't care. Sweeping aside the curtain he pushed the door, but it had been locked from the inside. He rattled the handle, but without result.

He slowly turned and crossed the floor to the exit. In the ante-room the man behind the cash desk was picking at his gleaming teeth with a pointed stick.

'I'd like to ask you a few questions about Meriol Stavanger if you wouldn't mind,' Jan said.

The man didn't respond.

'She's gone out', continued Jan, 'and locked the door to the dressing room.'

The man removed his tooth-pick and looked serious. 'You must not bother with the door, sir. I'm prepared to overlook what you did last time you were here, but you mustn't do anything like that again.'

Jan was silent for a moment, and the man resumed picking his teeth as if the conversation had ended satisfactorily.

'When will she come out again?' Jan asked.

'I don't know, sir.'

'Where does she live?'

'I don't know, sir.'

'But you must know,' Jan protested. 'She is employed here.'

The cashier laid the tooth-pick aside with the air of a man who was depriving himself of a particular pleasure. 'She is *not* employed here. She has permission to play the organ, and to sing here, but she is not employed here. She can come and go as she pleases.'

'At what times does she play?'

'It varies. She is a strange girl.'

'In what way is she strange?' asked Jan.

'She just is.'

Jan pondered before he asked the next question. 'Does she have many friends?'

'One or two perhaps.'

'Are they men or women?'

The man looked up, and his mouth gleamed in a wide grin. 'What do you mean?'

'I was thinking,' Jan said, and his breathing hurt him, 'that she seems very attached to the girl who is with her at the moment.'

'Very possibly. She is a strange girl. I told you she was a strange girl.'

Jan lit a felicity, walked back to the door, and looked into the darkened club. The organ stood in shrouded silence and there was no sign of Meriol. He imagined that the red velvet curtain moved, and then admitted that it was only his imagination which moved it.

The curtain hypnotized him. As he stared it became the veil which stood between himself and everything which was not himself, between the workings of his own consciousness and external reality, between the perceptions of his senses and the truth. It was the everlasting interface which could never be crossed.

Once again he imagined that the curtain moved. But he knew that behind the curtain was the door, and the door was locked from the other side.

He tried to close his mind to what might exist on the other side, and returned to the cash desk. The man looked up, with the tooth-pick sticking out of the side of his mouth like a dart. Jan placed the palms of his hands on the table and leaned forward with his weight upon them.

'Listen to me,' he said. 'I will give you anything, anything within my power, in return for the most minute piece of information about Meriol. Where she lives, where she goes, what time she comes here and what time she leaves, what she does, what her habits are, who her friends are, what they do. Anything. Do you understand? Absolutely anything.'

The cashier grinned so widely that he revealed the entry point of the tooth-pick between two bicuspids. 'I sympathize with your predicament, sir. But I can tell you nothing. Nothing at all. She is a perfect mystery. As I told you before, she is a strange girl.'

Jan looked hard into the grinning face, searching it for signs of duplicity. Then he straightened up, threw his felicity into an atomizer, and descended the precipitous stairs.

In Tubal Lane he felt like a fugitive, and knew that the punishment was greater than he could bear.

As he made his unseeing way through the black tunnel he thought of the two half-brothers descended from Cain: Jubal, who was the father of all such as handle the organ; and Tubal-cain, the instructor of every artificer in iron. Jubal and Tubal, ignorant of each other's features, were the Janus faces which looked in opposite directions upon the works of art and technology.

Jan turned to the right out of Vulcan Road into the thruway, and the dome of the Fun Palace loomed before him. He walked between the parallel rows of stylized trees up to the main entrance, and halted at one of the barriers. With nerveless hands he slapped his membership card on a plate where it was read by the flying spot of an alphanumeric scanner, and the barrier opened.

He squeezed through the narrow opening and made his way into the club. The Fun Palace was designed on lines which had become traditional in the larger clubs. In the centre was a small stage, from which tiered seats rose on all sides as in an amphitheatre. Between each circular tier of seats and the next was a continuous bar, broken only by escalators, equipped with the usual dispensing mechanisms for drinks and angel biscuits.

Where to sit was usually a question of general

strategy and personal preference, but tonight Jan went directly to the escalator opposite the main entrance. He stepped off into row F, the sixth from the top.

'Jan!' said the aphrodolly in seat number 249. 'You remembered!'

He sat down next to her without speaking.

'I told you I was always 'ere, didn't I?' She squeezed his fingers in her brown hand. 'But you might look a bit 'appier about it.'

Jan turned towards her. 'Anita. I need you to do something for me.'

'Of course, you silly boy,' she replied, widening her dark eyes. 'You've only got to ask.'

30

WHERE PEOPLE SAT in the Fun Palace, or in the other big clubs for that matter, depended upon their reason for going.

People who wanted to see the floor show sat in the lowest seats, near the small stage. This meant, however, that they were at the greatest distance from the aphrodollies, who congregated in the topmost tiers where they perched and twittered like migrant swallows. So those who came to talk to the aphrodollies naturally sat at the top.

But there was another factor. The aphrodollies sat at the top because there were no modesty panels under the dispensing counters which circled the top six tiers, and so they could signal with their flicker knickers to the largest possible audience.

Anyone who actually sat in the top six tiers ran the risk of not seeing the wood for the trees, as it were. Those who wished to select from an unrestricted field found it prudent to sit a little lower down, so that none of the signalling went unnoticed.

Consequently there was always a reasonable number of people around row K. Most of them were men who had saved up a whole year for the pleasures of this evening, and it would be another year before they could afford to come again. The teeming millions of Tcity, however, made it necessary for only a small fraction of the population to attend the clubs annually, in order to provide a continuous clientele.

In addition, of course, there was the much more frequent attendance by the hairdressers. Despite the widespread use of depilatory creams, wigs, and toupees, the long-standing failure to automate the cutting of hair had gradually elevated even routine barbers into a financial élite.

But all of these considerations were far away from the thoughts of Jan Caspol as he sat in row F next to the seat which Anita had vacated. He depressed the valve on his whisky flask, and stared at the stage with eyes which recorded without perceiving.

Naked sine notes from a music generator filled the amphitheatre, and their ubiquitous buzzing turned the cupola into a monstrous hive. A spotlight beamed onto the small, round stage, and into the circle of white light leapt a figure in armour.

The armour looked heavy, cruelly heavy, and it seemed scarcely possible that the wearer should be able to so much as raise an arm, or even crook a finger, within its riveted joints. But the cumbersome shape stood on its toes, and executed a series of *entrechat*, with the grace and buoyancy of a ballerina.

The figure raised an armoured fist, and with a deft movement removed the rounded helmet. A girl's face appeared, like Joan of Arc after the victory at Orleans, and she shook her golden hair free from the neck of the cuirass.

Jan thought of Brünnhilde, *schlafend ein won-niges Weib, in lichter Waffen Gewand.*

She began to pirouette, and as she spun round, the Missaglia-styled armour reflected the stage lighting in a dazzle of phosphorescent sparks. First she cast away one fingered gauntlet, and then the other. An electronic chord sounded and a mechanical voice began to sing.

> *Stahlex! Stahlex!*
> *Do you want it light?*
> *Do you want it bright?*
> *Do you want something that's nice and tight?*
> *Use stahlex! Use stahlex!*
> *A benevo—o—olent monopo—o—oly.*

The girl kicked off her ridged shoes, and skipped about the stage on bare feet. Then she flounced onto a stool, bent one leg and unstrapped the greave, bent the other leg and did the same. The greaves fell to the floor with a hollow, metallic tinkle.

> *Stahlex! Stahlex!*
> *Do you want it long?*
> *Do you want it strong?*
> *Do you want something that'll never go wrong?*
> *Use stahlex! Use stahlex!*
> *A benevo—o—olent monopo—o—oly.*

She danced about on legs that were bare beneath the knee, and returned to the stool. Pointing her toes towards the upper tiers of seats, she swivelled through a full circle in the opposite direction as she unbuckled the first cuisse, and swivelled through a full circle in the opposite direction as she unbuckled the other.

Stahlex! Stahlex!
Do you want it hot?
Do you want a lot?
Do you want something that'll never rot?
Use Stahlex! Use stahlex!
A benevo—o—olent monopo—o—oly.

The girl was now free of the legharness. Despite her sturdy thighs she looked top heavy, and as she pranced about she fiddled with some tapes under her arm. The shell-formed breastplate fell away with a clatter, and she was naked except for open-work bra and pants, computer-knitted out of fine gauge stahlex fibre.

Stahlex! Stahlex!
I want it thick!
I want it quick!
I want something that'll do the trick!
Use stahlex! Use stahlex!
A benevo—o—olent monopo—o—oly.

Jan decided that even Gerry Peters's latest gimmickry didn't make the waiting tolerable.

He began to will himself asleep, to obliterate the interval until Anita returned. Slowly and methodically he shut off the electrical impulses which stormed in his brain, retreating from consciousness like the sun from the day, or like a defeated general who spiked his forward guns before retiring behind his last line of defence.

31

ANITA WENT TO PULL open the second drawer of the cabinet, but impulsively changed her mind and opened the first. She scanned the index, inserted a finger, and extracted one of the blue data cards.

On the left-hand side were printed the statutory questions eliciting information for the General Register of Citizens, and on the right-hand side were her own handwritten responses.

Surname:
Other Names:
Height:
Hair:

Caspol
Jan
Slightly above average
Natural, dark

Her eyes ran down the other physical details, and then she turned over to look at the subjective data. She'd placed a tick well up on the aphrocollege's standard 10-point rating scale, which covered the whole spectrum from satyriasis to impotence, and in the spece provided for *General Comment* she'd written:

> *The above rating would be higher if he had not insisted that I turn off the aphrogas*

Anita's eyes traversed the rest of the card. Next to *Other Peculiarities* she'd put:

> *He does not like me to touch the sides of his head which seem to be a bit swollen above the ears*

She smiled as she replaced the card, closed the top drawer of the cabinet and opened the second one. The second drawer contained pink cards, and they were much fewer in number than the blue ones. She extracted a blank card, placed it on top of the cabinet, and made the first entries.

Surname:
Other Names:

Stavanger
Meriol

Anita filled in as many other physical details as she could. Looking pensively at the unanswered questions, she wondered what the card would look like in the morning when she filled in the empty spaces. Her hand hovered with the card above the alphabetical name tags, until she found the right place immediately in front of Steinberg.

She shuddered as she dropped the new card in place, and hoped tonight wouldn't be anything like that. It had required a second card, as an appendix, to cover all Val Steinberg's *Other Peculiarities*.

Anita stepped out of her clothes and switched on the aphrogas. After a moment's reflection she pulled on a simple dress, and crawled into the mouth of the aphrodome.

Meriol was lying there as if entranced, gazing at the stars with the wonder of a small girl staring at her first Christmas tree. The distant sound of sea waves kissing and sucking at the coral reef was like subdued music, and the air was redolent with the scents of sandalwood and island flowers. She turned her wide, round eyes to look at Anita.

'How nice it is!' Meriol murmured.

Anita slid up to her and looked down into her face. Meriol's upturned eyes were bright with the sparkle of reflected stars, and the natural pink of her lips was pale in the darkness. Anita stretched out a brown hand and stroked the girl's hair. The hair was straight, and cut without artistry, but it was wonderfully soft under her fingers.

Meriol's mouth quivered with a question, and the same question flashed in her eyes.

'Why did you want me to come with you?'

'Don't you know?'

Meriol lowered her eyes. 'I think so.'

Anita began to stroke her hair, but Meriol moved her head away and Anita dropped her hand to her side. There was silence for a few moments. Anita considered her mext move.

'Why did you want me to come?' Meriol asked again.

'Can't you guess?'

'I don't want to guess. I want you to tell me.'

Anita evaded. 'Why did you come with me? Was it because you liked me?'

'Ye-es.' It seemed a new idea to the girl. 'Partly.'

'Why did you like me?' coaxed Anita.

Meriol appeared to search for reasons. 'Because you were nice to me. You were nice when you came up to me in the club and said you liked my voice. People don't often do that.'

Anita gently placed her arm behind the girl's head. 'I think you 'ave a lovely voice. And I think you 'ave a lovely face. And I know that everything about you will be lovely.'

She felt Meriol stiffen against her arm. They were silent again, and the silence was perfect except for the distant sighing of the long waves and the whisper of the wind in the palm fronds as it distributed its heady burden of island perfumes and aphrogas.

'Are you glad you came?' asked Anita softly.

Meriol gazed at the stars, and nodded.

'And what was the other reason you came?' Anita asked. 'You said you came only partly because you liked me.'

'Yes. The main reason was that you said you were one of us, and that you had something to tell me.'

Anita leaned closer. 'I have.'

'What is it?'

'I don't think you know,' said Anita gently.

'No I don't. Tell me.'

'I don't know whether I dare.'

Meriol spoke impatiently. 'Of course you can. I'm one of you.'

Anita moved her arm downwards behind Meriol's head, until she could touch her opposite shoulder with her fingers. She put her head so close that when she spoke her lips brushed the girl's cheek.

'What are you thinking about?' she whispered.

Meriol sat up suddenly, and her shoulder pushed Anita's face away. Anita changed her tactics and lay down passively. Meriol supported herself on one hand and looked down at her.

'Tell me,' said Anita.

'I'm beginning to wonder whether you'd understand.'

'Try me,' Anita pleaded. 'You're one of us.'

Meriol's eyelids lowered. She scooped at the sand, and let the grains run through her fingers. She did it again. And again.

'Please,' Anita said.

'I was thinking about the way people used to be free,' Meriol replied.

'Free!'

'Yes. Do you ever think about the days when people used to be free?'

Anita was bewildered. 'But people are free now. They can do what they want.'

'No they can't,' Meriol contradicted. 'They can't go outside the cities. They can't go from one city to another, or go into the country, or go abroad. They can't do any work because there isn't any work for them to do. They can't vote for a different government. There's a lot of things they used to be able to do that they can't do now.'

Anita overcame her bewilderment. 'But that was ages ago', she said, 'and everybody knows that kind of freedom was no good. When ordinary folks like us used to vote for the Government, and used to work in factories, it was . . . ' She sought for some phrases which were conventionally used to describe the situation. 'It was absolute chaos in those days. Everybody knows that things are much better organized now.'

'Don't you think we've lost anything? Meriol

raised her eyes and looked at Anita intently.

'No. I know we 'aven't.'

'I told you that you wouldn't understand,' Meriol said. 'And do you know why you don't understand?'

'But I—'

'You don't understand', interrupted Meriol, 'because you're drugged. You're drugged like everybody else.'

Anita shrugged her shoulders. 'So they say. Some folk say it's in the water supply. But nobody thinks about it and I don't want to think about it.'

Meriol scooped at the sand again, and watched the grains run through her fingers.

'I thought you were one of us', she said, 'but you don't understand.'

'I do, I do,' Anita protested passionately.

She reached out, seized Meriol's hand, and pulled the girl towards her.

'I'm going to stroke you all over like a cat,' Anita said.

32

JAN CASPOL'S SELF-IMPOSED SLEEP was threaded
with dreams.

A figure appeared, clad in stahlex armour. It was
Meriol, he knew, because her voice sang through
the hinged vizor as clear and pure as a bird. He
rushed to embrace her, but the metal was as cold
as ice and froze his fingers.

With unsteady hands he began to strip the armour off—helmet, pauldrons, and vambraces. Inside there was another figure, also completely armoured. Meriol's voice continued to sing through
the vizor, but more softly than before.

Again he removed the armour, and again he
found an armoured figure inside. Meriol's voice
had become so faint that he had to put his ear
against the vizor to hear her song.

Once more he stripped the armour off, and once
more there was an armoured figure inside. The
singing had stopped. He placed his ear against the
vizor and held his breath.

'Hurry,' she whispered. 'You will soon have
solved the mystery.'

In a fevered torment he lifted off the helmet.

There was nothing inside. He was embracing a headless suit of miniature armour, and when he looked down into the black cavity of the collar he saw nothing. Very slowly he put his hand into the gaping aperture, then his forearm as far as the elbow, and then stretched until his arm was in up to the armpit and his fingers stroked the inside joints of the hollow legs. It was an empty shell.

With a groan of disappointment Jan awoke from his self-imposed sleep. A comedian occupied the small stage.

> *There was this young lass of fourteen you see. And she 'ad this old bloke of 'undred and four-teen come and stay with 'er in 'er module. Yes. A 'undred and fourteen. A young lass of four-teen and an old bloke of—*

Jan Caspol thought of Steinberg, and discovered that he envied him.

The pains and pleasures of the body for Stein-berg must by now be no more than lingering im-pressions scattered about his nervous system. His food, like that of the Sun King, was laced with sharper and sharper sauces, with increasing quan-tities of herbs and spices, with basil and garlic, with chillies, ginger, and black peppers, in desper-ate attempts to stimulate his waning taste buds.

> *And this other bloke in the next module 'ears these noises. Loud noises you see. Yes. Loud noises coming from this module where this young lass of fourteen is with this old bloke of—*

As far as wines were concerned, Steinberg had long since lost his ability to distinguish between

different years from the same vineyard, or between different vineyards in the same region. In
fact it was doubtful whether he could not tell the
difference between a hock from the Nahe and a
typical Moselle.

And so in the end this other bloke goes into the
module next door. He goes into the module
where this old bloke of 'undred and fourteen is
staying with this young lass of fourteen. Yes.
Young lass of—

And, inevitably, the sweetest of all the sensual
pleasures must now be without meaning for Steinberg. Injecting a phial of aphrojuice into his slug-
gish veins would be as pointless as pumping rocket
fuel into a Model-T Ford.

'No, I won't,' says the young lass of four-
teen, sitting tight on the lid of the thunder box.
'I've waited half the night', she says, 'to get
him in that state.'

The comedian bowed his way out to universal
applause, and the noise of the clapping hands and
cheering voices was deadened and made tolerable
by the sound-absorbent cladding of the amphitheatre. Jan looked at his chrono. He would
soon know the truth.

An aphrodolly passed by on the escalator, wearing a camelhair djellabah, and with her veil tied
behind the hood in the Tetuanese manner. The
upper tiers would be filling up by now.

An autocrooner moved onto the stage, flapping
a jointed foot on the floor to the rhythm of an
electric guitar, and levering its mechanical jaws in

phase with a pre-recorded dirge. Jan extracted his whisky flask and released the valve.

Replacing the whisky flask he saw Anita floating up towards him on the escalator. With a sensation of dread he searched her eyes for the truth to see if he could discover the worst before she spoke. She smiled and took her seat next to him.

'What happened?' he demanded. 'Tell me quickly. What happened? What happened?'

Anita patted his hand. 'Don't worry 'andsome boy.'

'What happened?'

'Nothing,' she said, and pointed to her eye. 'But there'll be a bruise 'ere tomorrow morning.'

Jan laughed out loud as he jumped to his feet. 'Where is she now?'

'Back at the Fiesta Club I suppose.'

He poured out incoherent thanks as he made his way to the escalator.

33

THE UPPER TIERS had indeed filled up. As Jan
Caspol was carried upwards on the escalator he
felt as if he was surveying the follies and lusts of all
mankind, from the dawn of civilization in the ancient river valleys to the present day. It was like
seeing an animated version of Chaucer's Legend of
Good Women, with scurrilous emendations and
additions by later hands.

Many of the aphrodollies made their appeal
through some historical gestalt. In addition to the
priestesses of Babylon and the hetaerae, the
houris and the geisha girls, the Victorian street-
walkers and demi-mondaines, and 20th-century
nymphets, there were numerous attempts at a
more individual representation.

Jan saw a palaeolithic woman, her body matted
with dank hair; Nefertiti, with her long neck and
serene beauty; Greta Garbo, with her Nordic
cheek-bones and broad shoulders.

In a small community of only a few million it
was possible for a man to feel isolated if his tastes
departed very far from the median. But in Tcity the
logic of large numbers gave every minority a social
and economic significance, and even the upper and
lower deciles were catered for.

And so it was that dotted here and there were grotesque succubi which looked as if they'd been fished out of the murkiest depths of Nero's subconscious. There were aphrodollies who were as thin as skeletons or as fat as pigs, whose faces showed the ravages of disease, who were ugly or deformed, who were without legs or had a supernumerary pair of arms; and other creatures into whom the skills of the genetic engineers had introduced additional X-chromosomes in order to produce the effects of Klinefelter's syndrome.

And on all sides, as Jan reached the top of the escalator, the flicker knickers signalled their invitations, as thickly clustered as stars at the centre of a galaxy.

Jan took the delevator down to the thruway, and pushed his way into Vulcan Road. The names of the narrow alleys were like obsolete words in an ancient text. He turned into Tubal Lane, and raced up the stairs of the Fiesta Club two at a time.

The man behind the pay desk looked up. 'Excuse me, sir. Excuse me.'

But Jan had hurried past without paying and entered the club room panting for breath. The organ was deserted. He crossed the room with rapid strides, swept the red velvet curtain aside, and tried the door. It was locked.

He rattled the handle in frustration, oblivious of the staring faces at nearby tables. With determination in his step he recrossed the room.

As he passed the table where they'd sat together the memory returned in all its painful detail. Once again he saw the shadows playing around her eyes and around her mouth. And once again there was something about the scene which appeared worthy of particular attention, but it was something which he couldn't quite identify.

He returned to the ante-room.

'Excuse me, sir. Excuse me.'

He went up to the cash desk. 'Where is she?'

'Excuse me, sir. I keep trying to tell you. Miss Stavanger asked me to give you this if you came back.'

The cashier held forward an envelope, and carefully inserted a sharpened piece of wood behind his eye tooth. Jan stared unbelievingly at the envelope for a few seconds, but then took it with an unsteady hand, turned it over, and retired a couple of paces.

The envelope was sealed, but without any writing on either side. He tore one corner, ripped it open with his finger, and flashed his eyes across the large, hurried scrawl.

> *You are in danger of being killed. Hide yourself in the city. If there is no other way spend the night with an aphrodolly. You can never see me again. Do not wait at the club because I shall never come back. Destroy this letter immediately.*

Jan walked over to the incinerator chute and was about to drop the letter in, when he realized that he couldn't bear to part with the only thing he had which reminded him of her. Opening the letter again he deliberated for a moment and tore out a small piece. He smiled as he read the fragment.

spend the night

with   *me*

The cashier was picking his teeth, his eyes fixed on space. Jan put the remains of the letter in the incinerator, and left the club. His thoughts were whirling in his head like dry leaves in an autumn wind.

The odds against finding Meriol in the city were millions upon millions to one. On the other hand, he reflected, if a man were sentenced to death with only one chance in a million million that he might escape, wouldn't he take that chance? Besides, his chances were better than that. At the very least he would find the spiral stairs which led down to the outside door of the dressing room.

As he shouldered his way back to the thruway, he sifted Meriol's message in his mind.

You are in danger of being killed. Why should anyone want to kill him? As far as he knew, he hadn't an enemy in the world. *Hide yourself in the city*. That was the most surprising part of the letter. Her advice that he should hide himself *in the city* seemed to imply that she knew he lived outside the city.

But that was impossible, he told himself, as he struggled into a levator station and forced his way into the required chamber. The minds of Citizens were conditioned by the drugs in the water supply, and they were unaware of the outside world.

If there is no other way spend the night with an aphrodolly. It was incredible, but those few words appeared to reveal a slight trace of jealousy. He would give anything, anything, to have the opportunity of proving to her that she need never have any cause to be jealous of anybody.

Jan was pushed out of the elevator into a crowded corridor, and took his bearings from the illuminated waymarks on the ceilings. It was several hundred metres to the narrow opening at the top of the spiral stairway, but he had something to occupy his thoughts in the meantime.

You can never see me again . . . Destroy this letter immediately. She was warning him of some kind of plot against his life, even though she put herself in danger by doing so. His heart moved with a sensation of love and pain.

If Meriol was putting herself in danger by warning him, he reasoned, then it was because she possessed secret information which she wasn't supposed to use. This secret information might have been acquired accidentally, or it might have been generated by a society to which she belonged.

He wondered again why anyone should want to kill him. If there wasn't any reason why anybody should want to kill him as an individual, there might still be a reason why somebody should want to kill him as a member of a class. As an Executive.

As he walked along, the crowded corridor with the scented air from the blowers spreading the hair across his forehead, he remembered the shabby figure near the terminus of the thruway, and suddenly felt cold.

He turned to look at the scurrying people around him, to see whether they were noticing the cold, and the blow was like a bomb exploding inside his head.

Buckling at the knees, he saw that he was falling against the wall next to a retrieval panel. He'd no sooner discovered the fortunate coincidence than he realized he would not have the strength to press the button. But he needn't have worried.

A shabby figure leaned over and pressed the retrieval button for him. Jan keeled over, and the man roughly kicked him into alignment with the wall. Far, far away, at the very edges of perception, Jan was aware of a high-pitched whistle which interrupted a pale blue silence. His eyes remained open long enough to see the man take something from his shabby coat, and the second blow snapped the remaining shreds which connected him to consciousness.

34

NICK LEVANTINE TOOK his accustomed seat in the Blue Star Club. Someone had been sitting there before him and the dispensing counter was littered with the remains of angel biscuits. It was sufficient, he reflected, as he swept the crumbs away with his hand, to destroy any ambition a man might have to get to Heaven.

He raised the opera glasses and surveyed the top tiers on the other side of the amphitheatre. She wasn't there. Ignoring the flickering signals he traversed impatiently to the right, and then to the left. There she was!

Nick lowered the opera glasses and got to his feet. As he did so he suddenly remembered Steinberg's request for Henry's recording tapes. Damn! He'd been so anxious to get away from Wilkie that he'd forgotten all about them. He directed his course behind the top tiers of seats, and he told himself that it didn't matter. Steinberg would have to wait until tomorrow morning.

The aphrodolly looked up as he approached, and she looked even better than he remembered her from three evenings ago. It was as if she had been put together specifically to please him.

'Hiya, Linda,' he said.

Her full mouth parted in a smile of welcome as he sat beside her.

Nick lounged with one arm round her shoulders, and used his other hand to ply the whisky flask. After a while something caught his attention on the other side of the amphitheatre not far from where he'd been sitting. He lowered his flask to the dispensing counter, and raised the opera glasses.

'You're being very rude,' Linda said.

He continued to scowl through the glasses, and anger made him pale.

'What's the matter?' asked Linda. 'Are you dissatisfied with me already, or are you only trying to make me jealous?'

She leaned her head on his shoulder, and her rich, auburn curls caressed his cheek. Nick lowered the glasses and kissed her viciously on her voluptuous mouth.

'Let's go,' she said.

That was exactly what Nick wanted to do, but he was surprised by her impatience. 'Do you want to go now?'

'Yes.' She returned the kiss. 'Besides, it's getting cold in here. Do you feel cold?'

Curiously enough, it had turned rather cold.

Linda bent her head and looked at the chrono on his wrist. 'Let's go,' she repeated.

Nick drained his whisky, flung the empty flask into a disposal chute, and willingly followed her to the escalator.

He couldn't be sure about the veiled woman in the djellabah. But he didn't want to sit there any longer with those sombre eyes watching him.

35

THE COLOURS WERE olive green, vermilion, and purple, and as the symmetries changed their relationships the colours often shaded into black. But there had been an interruption, and as the colours faded away Steinberg discovered that he was staring at the wall, with Webern's Variations for piano, op. 27, tracing aural patterns on his brain.

The interruption had been caused by another sound, which slowly became identified as the buzzing of the video.

Steinberg flicked a switch, and a thin, worried face appeared on the screen. It was a nondescript, ordinary sort of face.

'Who are you?' demanded Steinberg. 'What do you want?'

'I'm Fred, sir.'

'Who?'

'Fred, sir. The Fred what's in the south Gatehouse, sir. The Fred what looks after the young gentlemen's needs when they feel inclined to what some folk call—'

'Idiot!' Steinberg's fury almost choked him. 'Idiot! Half-wit! How dare you intrude yourself upon me! Lunatic!'

'I'm terribly sorry, sir, and I wouldn't for all the world, sir, if I didn't think it was important, sir, but there's men on the other side of the Gatehouse, sir, and I—'

Steinberg felt the veins popping on the sides of his head. 'Fool! How dare you contact me with such irrelevant information! I shall have you removed.'

'I'm frightened, sir. The men on the other side of the Gatehouse seem to be waiting for something and I know it's a terrible thing to ask, sir, and I only mention it because I'm so frightened, sir, but if anything dreadful 'appens can I borrow one of the young gentlemen's autos, sir, but only if—'

'You are not to so much as touch an auto under any circumstances whatsoever,' squeaked Steinberg. 'You are to stay precisely where you are until you are replaced, which will be as soon as I can possibly arrange it.'

As Steinberg cleared the screen he was painfully aware of the pulses above his ears.

36

WHEN JAN CASPOL opened his eyes he was lying
on a spartan bed next to the wall in a small cell. The
walls were made from stahlex sheets, stark and
plain, and their smooth surfaces were unbroken
except for a row of three coloured buttons on the
other side of the cell. Facing the door, completely
immobile and with its back towards him, stood a
cyborg.

With an immense effort of will Jan set about
overcoming his amnesia, and he began by concen-
trating on the cyborg.

The cyborgs were built by GK under licence
from Cyborghandlung Gesellschaft and they were
beautiful pieces of biomechanical engineering, although the widely advertized use of brains from St
Bernard dogs was said to be something of a gim-
mick. The equipping of the retrieval systems in the
city corridors had resulted in the largest cyborg
order ever placed in Europe.

All the main corridors of the city were provided
with retrieval depots at intervals of 1,000 metres,
and each depot had a minimum complement of one
cyborg and a maximum complement of two. The
cyborgs were constantly moving from one depot to

the next, empty-handed if necessary, in order to maintain this balance. They always moved in the direction of the traffic flow, and there was consequently a steady transfer of cyborgs through the levator stations at the extreme ends of the main corridors as they went up or down to another floor to recommence operations in the opposite direction.

Jan's thoughts were abruptly redirected by an electroluminous sign which blinked on over the door.

Doctor Coming

He tried to sit up, but a painful throbbing in his head made him fall back again. Lifting his hands, he explored two bumps on the back of his cranium. Apart from those, everything appeared to be in order. There didn't seem to be anything missing, but he found a shred of paper in his pocket with some words scrawled by a rapid pen.

spend the night

with

me

His mind picked up the association, dropped it, and then circled until it was recovered, like a well-trained dog on the track of a half-remembered scent. Starting from Meriol's letter he began to move forwards through time, little by little reconquering the memories he had lost.

He recalled his journey along the corridor, the blow on his head, the lucky coincidence of falling next to a retrieval panel. Jan's head throbbed as he instructed his brain to recapitulate the last seconds before he lost consciousness, and the sweat came out on his brow as the last synapses closed in his memory circuits.

When the gap had been filled he knew that it wasn't coincidence at all. He had been deliberately struck down next to a panel so that he could be collected without inconvenience and brought to this retrieval depot.

Jan looked at the cyborg. It remained perfectly motionless, facing the door. All its systems were off, and it would presumably not move until there was either a retrieval call in the direction of the traffic flow, or a cyborg arrival from the other direction. When either of these things happened, and one or other of them was bound to happen sooner or later, the door must open and Jan thought he might be able to slip out.

The door, of course, might open for a third reason. Jan raised his eyes to the electroluminous sign. *Doctor Coming,* and reflected that the assurance must have revived the spirit of many a Citizen lying on this bed with broken bones. But he recalled Meriol's warning, and decided that his attacker hand't arranged for him to be brought to this depot for purposes connected with his personal welfare. Jan concluded that he couldn't afford to run the risk that the third reason for the door opening might operate first.

He forced himself to sit up, and swung his legs over the edge of the bed. The splitting pain in his head disoriented his faculties slightly, and he thought the cyborg was beginning to turn. But it remained stationary.

Jan looked past the cyborg's shoulders at the door, and his eyes traced the hair-line cracks where it slid into place. It was obvious that any thought of forcing the stahlex panel was hopeless.

He switched his scrutiny to the walls, where his gaze came to rest on the only item which broke their smooth surface: the three buttons. With silent movements he slithered from the bed, and the moment his feet touched the floor a jab of pain travelled up his spine and lodged under his skull.

Jan examined the three buttons. What he wanted was a button which would open the door, but there was no inscription to indicate their purpose.

He decided upon a simple strategy. First he would press the button on the left, and wait for a moment to see if anything happened. If the door opened he would slip round the cyborg into the corridor. If the door didn't open he would assume that he'd activated some other system inimical to himself, and press the second button. And so on to the third, if necessary.

Pressing the first button he turned to regard the door. Nothing happened. He was about to press the second button when his eyes ceased to register the electroluminous sign over the door. The panel where the message had been was a grey blank. Within a moment the cyborg stepped sideways and the door opened to reveal three men, one of them carrying a surgical bag.

Jan pressed the second and third buttons simultaneously. As the three men entered the cell a panel opened in the wall, and he dived headlong into it.

Then he was falling, falling.

37

IT WAS A FEW SECONDS before Jan Caspol realized that he wasn't actually falling through space, but that he was speeding feet first down a steeply inclined surface. Raising his hands, he discovered that there was nothing above his head except the impenetrable blackness. When he lowered his hands they came into contact with the sides of the chute down which he was travelling.

After a few minutes the downward gradient became less steep, and he began to move more slowly. Then without warning the left-hand side of the chute disappeared, and for one searing fraction of a second he once again thought he was falling through space. But the side of the chute reappeared immediately, and gave him a tingling blow on his projecting elbow.

Another gap occurred on the right-hand side, and the moment after he passed, something bulky shot out of it into the chute, chased after him, caught him up, and started to beat against his back. Jan twisted round, lashed out, and managed to get hold of a fistful of coarse, long hair. Determined to inflict pain on the aggressor, he twisted the hair as hard as he could.

Almost immediately, however, there was a dull thud ahead of him as another creature issued from a gap on the left, and crawled onto his feet. Jan kicked out with all his strength and the second assailant slid away from him.

The first attacker didn't appear to be putting up any vigorous defence. With sudden insight Jan released the hair, and his fingers explored the cold, wrinkled face of an old woman.

In the meantime he'd caught up again with the object travelling in front of him, and when he stretched forward he found a pair of legs as straight and stiff as sticks.

The thuds became more frequent, both in front and behind, and the chute broadened out. It became obvious to Jan that he was now travelling down a main conveyor, fed by tributary chutes from which the bodies catapulted like rabbits frightened out of their holes by a roving ferret. And it became equally clear that he was an item of cargo in an extensive underground network; and that the network was collecting the bodies of those who had been unfortunate enough to stumble in the city corridors, and be retrieved by the cyborgs.

The conveyor levelled out further and the speed continued to decrease. More corpses slapped into the sliding column. A heavy man plummeted straight into Jan and fell across his chest, followed promptly by a gangling youth who still reeked of alcohol.

Jan suddenly realized that he was in danger of being suffocated, and he struggled with the dead men until he was on top.

Imperceptibly, the darkness began to lighten. Jan thought he was imagining it at first, but illuminations appeared, adding a spectral air of festival to the buildings ahead.

He got to his knees and then to his feet, supporting himself with his hands on the sides of the conveyor. It would have been impossible to remain upright on the polished stahlex surface, had there not been fleshy cushions to stand upon.

Jan looked over the side. The conveyor was now fairly near the ground, and supported on a lattice of stahlex sections. He looked ahead and saw that the conveyor entered a circular tunnel, cut into the end of a long, narrow building, from which a series of chimneys projected.

He waited a little longer, They were all moving very slowly.

With the entrance to the tunnel only a few metres away he gathered his strength, pulled himself up the side of the conveyor, and swung astride the edge. After pausing a few seconds to regain his breath he lowered himself on the other side, hung by his hands, pushed away slightly to avoid the supporting lattice, and dropped.

Jan gauged the drop carefully, allowing his legs to absorb the impact like springs under compression. The ground was hard, however, and it flung him sideways, almost at the feet of the two men who were waiting under the conveyor for him.

'Dead on time,' one of them said, standing back a pace and pointing a gun.

'Not quite, but we'll soon be on schedule,' joked the other, and seized Jan by the arms. 'It's these that we've been waiting for.'

It would be a little time before Jan understood why the man had grabbed his arms with such proprietary zeal, almost as if he were a starving man selecting two long-desired items of butchers meat.

PHILLIPPA WAS GLAD of the djellabah, because without it she would have been cold.

She continued to sit in the upper tiers of the Blue Star Club, with the tears pricking at the corners of her powdered eyes, and the thoughts cascading inside her brain like tinsel in a kaleidoscope.

What will become of me? she thought. What shall I do?

The rest of her life appeared before her like an empty road which led from now to nowhere, an unused data bank which would never contain anything worthy of recall.

She couldn't believe it was happening to her.

Memories of Nick's face, when he ripped the black mask away yesterday, and when he suspected her identity this evening, were interwoven with every living impulse of her body. With despair she admitted to herself that she would rather see him despising her, would rather see him kissing the woman with the auburn curls, than not see him at all.

Phillippa cried, and her veil was stained by the kohl in her coursing tears.

THE REBELLIOUS MOB was packed into the waste land of the compound as densely as matter in a collapsed star, and the northbound paveline of Thruway 1 brought a continuous stream of reinforcements.

Inside the south Gatehouse stood a man with an amputated left arm in his hands. He held it diagonally across his chest. Experiment had quickly shown the angle at which the arm should be held in order that the Executive code would operate the receptors in the door jambs. Sometimes the man's shoulders would droop with fatigue, and then the door would partially close before angry shouts made him straighten up again.

The mob trouped through the Gatehouse in an unending column, sometimes pausing to kick the gilt legs of the Louis XVI furniture, spit on the chaise longue, or make jokes about Fred's insatiable taste for the good life.

Fred sat stiffly in the Poirié chair, with his head thrown back and his mouth stretched open to its widest extent in order to accommodate a bottle of his favourite Alsatian wine. The wine had flowed through his broken teeth and down his chin, and the red bubbles would have puzzled any connoisseur who failed to realize that the bottle had been pushed down Fred's throat until its long, elegant neck had poked a hole in his wind-pipe.

At the other side of the Gatehouse stood a man who held a right arm diagonally across his chest, and who kept asking plaintively for someone to relieve him.

Far away, at the north Gatehouse, a detached pair of plump white arms was performing a similar function.

Val Steinberg's arms had embraced an immense variety of objects in their time, but even they had never before kept open house to such a multitude of men and women.

40

'WALK!' COMMANDED THE FIRST MAN, gesturing with his gun.

The other man led the way and Jan followed. Behind him was the conveyor, with its endless freight sliding into the circular tunnel like a train of canal barges. In front of him were office buildings whose lighted windows shone like burnished shields on a blackened wall.

The man in front opened a door and went inside. Jan followed, with the gun prodding his ribs, along a glazed passage with rooms leading off it. One of the rooms appeared to contain temperature and pressure gauges with graduated dials and other primitive control devices.

They came to a heavy door at the end of the passage. The man in front knocked, went in, and closed the door behind him. Jan turned his head to observe his surroundings more closely, but the gun nozzle bruised against his ribs.

'Keep still.'

The door re-opened.

'Bring him in,' called a new voice.

Jan entered a room which was excessively large by city standards. On his right was a window which threw a rectangle of light into the darkness outside. In a corner was an old-fashioned filing cabinet on which stood a stahlex figure similar to the one in the dressing room at the Fiesta Club. In front of him was an antique steel desk, and behind the desk was a man whose face he'd seen before.

The man behind the desk looked past Jan's shoulders. 'You can both go back to your duties.'

'Excuse me, sir, but are you sure—'

'Go back to your duties,' he repeated.

The two men went out and Jan breathed more easily.

'It was foolish of you to think you could get away. I was aware that you were on your way here, as it were, within seconds of your escape from our surgeon.'

'At least it brought me to someone I've met before,' Jan countered.

'So you remember me?'

'Yes.' Jan would have remembered that sad face even if it hadn't been for the recent wound on the right cheek. 'What I can't understand is how you avoided being processed in your own water reclamation plant.'

The young man closed his paper-thin eyelids as if in pain. 'We aren't so desperate as you seem to imagine. Only the dead are put into the chutes. But the dead are very numerous, and over two thirds of each body is reducible to water, so we have an unadulterated supply sufficient to maintain our forces.'

Jan was puzzled. 'But what do your forces, as you call them, hope to achieve? What do you want?'

'You wouldn't understand,' was the bitter reply.

'Surely you're not a reactionary,' Jan said. 'Surely everyone knows that the old egalitarian systems, the old democracies, were hopelessly inefficient and stupid. All you've got to do is read the history books.'

The man leaned across his desk. 'Perhaps the old systems were inefficient, but they embodied more justice than the present one.'

'But the old systems were based on lies,' Jan protested, incredulous that anyone should attempt to argue the point. 'The situation in industry and politics was absolutely hopeless, and it became clear to everyone that we couldn't afford to let ordinary people have any say in how things were organized. There used to be industrial strikes, sabotage of computer centres, demands for equal privileges, and . . . '

Jan waved his arm, to encompass the mountainous idiocy of previous ages, and discovered that without intending to he'd indicated the stahlex figure on top of the filing cabinet.

'And creative activity,' completed the man behind the desk, 'of which some of us are once again capable.'

A harsh buzz issued from a speaker on the steel desk, and the man leaned forward to depress a lever.

'Everything is going according to plan,' announced a voice. 'We have secured two pairs of—'

The young man quickly depressed another lever and lifted the receiver to his ear, so that he would listen to the message in private. But Jan had heard sufficient to recognize the voice.

'Good,' said the man behind the desk. 'Excellent.'

As he listened to the next words he looked at Jan with wrinkled brows.

'Yes,' he said in response to a question. 'He's

been on our water for several weeks. I'll tell you now.'

He laid the receiver on the desk and crossed to the filing cabinet. With quick fingers he found what he wanted, scribbled a note, and returned to the speaker. Jan listened as an address in the Second Sector was given. The speaker was without video, but Jan had no difficulty in visualizing the exophthalmic eyes of Bendix.

The conversation ended, and the young man replaced the receiver.

'I think your actions are based on envy,' Jan said.

'Quiet!' the man behind the desk started to shout, and his prematurely aged face twisted with an ungovernable anger which showed, clearly enough, that Jan had hit upon the truth. 'You are not our superiors by nature. By moral and artistic standards you are actually our inferiors. And if it hadn't been for a father who was so besotted with his own pride that he thought I would inherit his artificial intelligence . . .'

He regained sufficient control of his feelings, cut short his outburst, and he continued in a lowered voice.

'Partly because you are no longer necessary to our project, and partly because I cannot overcome a feeling of gratitude to you, I am going to tell you how to escape. But don't provoke me, or I may change my mind.'

He paused to assemble his thoughts. For a moment the deep wrinkling of his brows struck Jan with a sense of familiarity. It was a familiarity which antedated the face of a man who had stumbled in a city corridor only an evening before.

'I shall leave this room', he continued, 'and go

into the office of my works manager, who is the only person who can see the levator door from his window. While I engage his attention with some reports on the other side of his office, you will leave this room and take the levator. The levator door is opened by a combination lock and the number is 57843.

'Thank you,' Jan said.

'You'll have no difficulty in remembering the number sequence with your perfect memory.' His face was lined with venom. 'But if you want a mnemonic it's the mean solar distance of Mercury in thousands of kilometres.'

'Thank you,' said Jan, again. 'I know it sounds inadequate, but I'm most sincerely grateful to you for—'

The other man raised a hand to stop any further expressions of thanks, which were clearly unwelcome to him.

'Give me three minutes and then leave,' he said, as he turned towards the door. 'Hide yourself in the city.'

The door closed behind him, and the unconscious echo of the advice in Meriol's letter conjured up the picture which haunted Jan like a recurring dream. Once again he watched the candle-light licking at her eyelids, her small freckled nose, the lobes of her ears, and he saw the darkness come and go under her bottom lip.

But now he was able to focus on the detail which had previously eluded him. The fruit juice in her glass was untouched, just as his own beer was untouched.

Jan strode rapidly to the old-fashioned filing cabinet in the corner of the room, and re-opened the drawer which had been pulled open only a few minutes earlier. He immediately came across the file of addresses and quickly found what he was looking for. Meriol's address was module 7, vestibule 130, corridor 361, floor 3, Second Sector.

He crossed behind the antique steel desk. Its working surface was littered with the impedimenta of obsolete commercial practices: pens, pencils, paper clips, elastic bands, a slide rule, a calculating machine, and a graph of water output showing hectalitres produced per eight-hour shift. Scattered about were memoranda and scribbled pieces of paper.

Jan riffled through a handful of memoranda in the in-tray. They were all addressed to the same person. Paul Steinberg.

He went out. In the passage he had a brief glimpse of Paul Steinberg and another man with their backs to the office window, poring over some columns of figures on lined paper. The other man was adding the figures up, and jotting notes on a scribble pad.

The novelty of the scene enchanted Jan, but he moved on to the levator door. He promptly ran through the number sequence on the combination dial and the door opened.

41

THE NEXT TIME the colours faded Steinberg discovered that the music of Webern was being drowned by a high-pitched alarm note. He twisted round, and stared with incredulity at some bright red lettering which had appeared on the display screen.

works on stop

He stared at the screen for a long time, incapable of action, while the blood hammered through the passageways above his ears. Finally he made himself speak.

'Message received,' he said.

But Steinberg's voice had issued as no more than a whisper, and it wasn't picked up by the audio receivers.

'Message received,' he repeated, more loudly.

The display screen blanked, and the high-pitched alarm note cut off in the same instant. Steinberg turned towards the video.

'Get me Levantine,' he instructed.

The small screen illuminated and presented a message.

regret mr levantine not available

Steinberg turned back to the display screen.

'Put me in control of the works management support system,' he commanded.

go ahead

'Why is the works on stop?' he asked.
The answer came immediately.

insufficient orders

'What!'
The exclamation had left Steinberg's mouth with explosive force, but it was treated by the audio receivers as an interrogative. Consequently the screen blanked, and represented its message.
'I want some more details,' Steinberg hissed. 'Explain what is meant by insufficient orders.'

> *order load has fallen below critical level required to maintain a single storage sphere on stream without transgressing heat-sinking safety parameters. metals plant has therefore been taken out of commission.*

'Put me through to Caspol,' he said.
The video winked at him.

regret mr caspol not available

Steinberg returned to the large screen. 'Put me in control of the sales management support system.'

go ahead

'Show me the current order position,' he demanded.

The statistical table appeared, with the names of Consumers listed in the first column. Steinberg's eyes moved from left to right over the data. During the previous twenty-four hours GK and Groundcars had placed a few insignificant orders and nobody else had ordered anything. The final column showed an unbroken series of large negative divergences.

Steinberg squeezed the sides of his chair until his fingers ached. He told himself that this was a nightmare in which he was forced to play this farcical rôle until he awoke.

'Fade,' he said.

The screen blinked and presented the statistical table for Stockholders. Steinberg's eyes looked up and down the columns of figures like weary travellers searching for a lodging and finding none. Only Wales Stockholders had ordered anything at all.

'Fade,' he said weakly, and turned to the video. 'Get me . . . get me Tilling of Aerospace.'

The screen illuminated, and after a short interval Mr Tilling appeared, sleepy-eyed, and drawing together the collar of what looked like a silk dressing gown.

'Mr Steinberg!' he exclaimed. 'This is a pleasant surprise. *Welch' Licht leuchtet dort? Dämmert der Tag schon auf?*'

Steinberg ignored the Wagnerian greeting and came straight to the point. 'Why didn't you place any orders yesterday?'

'Why?' Mr Tilling smiled. 'Because David Bendix, the new man at North Eastern Stockholders, came through to me and asked if I could take some surplus stock off his hands.'

Steinberg felt a pulse start to beat painfully in the sides of his head. 'But did that cover all your requirements?'

'Yes. All my current requirements. Bendix said that when he took over North Eastern Stock-holders he discovered that they were grossly over-stocked in everything, and that it would help him to run his stocks down to a reasonable level if I took a day's usage.'

Steinberg's face set in graven lines as if it had been hacked out of granite.

'It won't cause you any inconvenience will it, Mr Steinberg? The supply system is self-adjusting, and with an economy in equilibrium you won't—'

'Idiot!' gasped Steinberg, and disconnected.

The word associated itself in Steinberg's mind with a thin, worried face, and he issued another command.

'Get me the south Gatehouse.'

The screen shimmered. There were indistinct signs of movement, and then a pale, unfamiliar face swam into focus.

Steinberg was taken aback. 'Where's . . . where's Fred?'

'Fred? Who's Fred? You mean the Gatehouse keeper? I'm afraid 'e's not available. Not available at all, isn't Fred. Fred's been 'itting the bottle a bit too 'ard. In fact 'e's—'

The man was unable to maintain the pretence of respectful attention any longer and burst into help-less laughter. Another face appeared on the screen.

'Who's that fat slug?' asked the newcomer.

Steinberg opened and closed his mouth convul-sively, like a stranded fish.

Another head pushed its way onto the video.

'Whoever you are, we're on our way to get you.'

A swinging bottle appeared, travelling towards Steinberg's face. The video picture shattered and became silent.

Steinberg sat as immobile as an obelisk for a few seconds, while the pulses above his ears clanged like brass cymbals. He tried to raise the north Gatehouse without success.

'Put me in contact with Miss Steinberg,' he instructed.

The message on the video was the one he expected.

regret miss steinberg not available

'Put me in control of the city engineering support system,' he instructed.

The voice frequency analyzer in Val Steinberg's empty systems lounge verified the authority of her father's voice.

go ahead

Steinberg leaned forward with pain to issue his last command.

42

THE BUTTON PANEL covered most of the side wall above waist height, making Jan feel that he was in the control cockpit of some unfamiliar machine. He surveyed the studded surface, and soon found the numbered button he was looking for near the left-hand bottom corner. The private levator promptly whisked him upwards.

The ascent was long. He wondered whether the levator might be over-shooting, until he recalled that the water reclamation plant was subterranean.

He stepped out into a crowded corridor, and the levator door snapped shut behind him. Looking up at the ceiling waymarks he saw that he was indeed on floor 3 in the Second Sector, and in corridor 350.

Jan began to traverse the corridors of floor 3. It was now quite cold, and he noticed some people walking with their hands in their pockets. He would have liked to do the same, but decided it was much too dangerous a practice. Anyone who fell with his hands in his pockets, and failed to withdraw them before he hit the floor, would have virtually no chance of survival.

Besides, he might need his hands to defend himself, especially as the Second Sector was obviously a dormitory area for the forces of rebellion.

His head started to throb again where he'd received the double blow. In his weariness the corridor appeared to incline upwards, and then downwards, and then to waver like a vision in a mirage. He turned into another corridor, and for a dizzying moment he couldn't remember the number of the corridor he'd just left.

Sometimes he thought he was going in the wrong direction. Sometimes he imagined that he was passing waymarks for the second time, and that he was trapped in a loop.

It seemed to him that this cold, perfumed ozone had been blowing in his face for as long as he could remember, and that he was condemned to walk along these corridors for ever. These corridors and vestibules weren't pathways to anywhere, but a maze in which the ariadne thread had broken, a medina of the mind where he was searching around the labyrinthine windings of his own brain.

He didn't seem to be moving. He was caught like a wingless fly in the deepest recesses of a gigantic honeycomb. He was committed to an endless journey, like a microbe in the bowels of leviathan.

It wasn't until he actually entered corridor 361 that he was able to believe in the progress he had made. He glanced at the waymarks, and saw that the even-numbered vestibules were on his left and the odd numbers on his right. With increasing excitement he began to edge towards the left-hand wall as he walked, ready for the turning into vestibule 130.

Jan tried to hurry, but the crowd was too dense.

He was impatient, now, and nobody was moving quickly enough.

As he was passing the junction with vestibule 126 the ozone breeze freshened. He thought it must be a short squall, due to some trick of the air currents or some random oscillation in a blower. Within a few more steps, however, the breeze had turned into a steady wind which would have registered Force 6 on the Beaufort Scale, and its energy was increasing every second.

Long screams echoed through the corridor, bouncing from kilometre to kilometre along the angled vestibules and the perfumed air vibrated with nibelung cries of terror. Jan looked at his chrono in disbelief.

It was much too early for the Curfew, but there could be no doubt about what was happening. The scavenger system was in operation.

The crowds split, and started to disappear like winnowed chaff into the adjoining vestibules. Jan saw his way clear, and tried to run into the wind, but the wind was more of an obstacle than the crowds had been.

As he was passing the junction with vestibule 128 the cross-wind from a transverse blower threw him to his knees in the middle of the corridor. He looked sideways.

In the vestibule almost every door had been opened by the occupants, and complete strangers were scrambling into the safety of the modules. When he looked ahead he saw the the main corridor was now completely deserted, and its empty perspective disappeared into infinity.

The wind had risen to a gale, and he didn't dare attempt to stand up again. He decided, in any case, that it was better to crawl, because by doing so, he offered less wind resistance.

The litter and rubbish of the previous day, collected from greater and greater distances, was scurrying towards him. Most of it passed him by, but dust blew into his eyes, nose, and throat, and streamers of paper wound round his arms and legs where they rippled in the wind like pennons.

When he looked forward through streaming eyes he saw the waymarks pointing across to vestibule 130. It was only another few metres, but the air blast now had the force of a hurricane and pressed him flat to the floor. He feared that at any moment he would lose his adhesion to the floor and be swept along with the debris of the departed day.

The floor beneath his nose began to flash pale blue and from the empty reaches of the corridor ahead he heard an intermittent whistle. The whistle rapidly came nearer, accompanied by the sound of widely spaced, heavy footsteps.

He looked up and saw a retrieval cyborg, which had been turned round by the wind, running helplessy down the corridor with the hurricane behind it.

The cyborg's homing functions were presumably in disarray, but its alarm systems were going full blast. As Jan watched, however, it became evident that the St Bernard brain still had some kind of rapport with the retrieval bio-mechanisms.

The cyborg crossed to his side of the corridor, and bent almost double until it was on the point of overbalancing. Its long arms were held forward like scoops, with the obvious intention of scraping Jan off the floor as it ran past.

Jan's eyes were squeezed shut, and his jaws stiff

with determination, as he tortured his body forward. He crawled until he was able to clamp his
numb hands on the corner of the vestibule.

The cyborg was almost on top of him, and
crouched lower, with its extended forearms
scratching the floor. Jan's biceps almost burst as he
hauled himself around the corner into the vestibule.

But he didn't get completely around the corner,
because he experienced a glancing blow against
his instep. The cyborg's foot had only just touched
him as it hurtled past, but it was sufficient to upset
the precarious balance of the heavy machine.
There was a resounding clatter. The cyborg rolled
away down the corridor with flailing arms and
flashing lights, and its whistle slowly faded in the
thinly perfumed wind.

Jan crawled forward into the blast from the
transverse blower. There was nobody in the vestibule. He rested for a few seconds outside module
2, but he knew he was weakening and that he
couldn't afford to linger. At module 4 he left the
wall and began to cross over.

The hurricane lifted him, and moved him back a
couple of metres. He lay on his stomach, and
pressed his cold, unfeeling fingers against the
floor. Slowly, carefully, he edged forward again.

He knocked on the bottom of the door to module
7. Nothing happened. He knocked again.

The hurricane seemed to blow with renewed
force. Jan's cold fingers began to slip, and he tried
to gain some kind of hold with his finger nails in the
hair-line crack which edged the door. He knew
that he was in the position of a suspended climber
who sees the fraying rope begin to part.

With everything that was left of his strength he beat despairingly on the bottom of the door. The door opened a few centimetres, and he found himself looking at a row of small, white toes.

43

WHEN THE SCAVENGER SYSTEM started to operate, Phillippa was on her way back to the Gatehouse. She was travelling on the slow lane of the northbound paveline in Thruway 1. Love, shame, and despair had so clouded her perceptions that she didn't realize what was happening until the stampede began.

The more thinly populated southbound paveline slowed down, and after a few seconds it stopped. The people travelling on it looked round with expressions of astonishment. It was the first time any of them had experienced a mechanical failure.

The southbound paveline then started to move backwards, and quickly speeded up until both the south and northbound pavelines were accelerating in a parallel line towards the terminus, and at the same time the southerly breeze was whipped up into a gale. There was total panic.

Those who reacted quickly enough, and who were well-positioned, threw themselves from the accelerating pavelines into the sidewalks. The old and the infirm were thrust aside, pushed over, and trampled underfoot. Phillippa was swept from the slow lane and found herself in the middle of a shrieking, fear-crazed mob which battered at the doors of the beeblocks.

People fought each other to get inside. Those already inside were trying to close the doors in the faces of those who were following, but the external pressure was too strong.

Phillippa was part of a screaming mob which swayed and surged outside one of the open doors. Her veil had been torn from her face, and unseen hands swung her round by her hood. She struggled out of the heavy djellabah to avoid being choked, and felt herself pushed backwards into the crowd.

She saw the pavelines sliding past. They were relatively deserted now, and all the passengers were involuntary. There were the prostrate shapes of those who had been knocked unconscious or killed in the rush to safety, and the more clamorous figures of those whom the hurricane had detached from the inadequate sidewalks.

A stray cat sailed by, sitting motionless, enjoying the ride and the unwonted sensation of space.

Suddenly one of the prostrate shapes on the paveline got to its knees, stood up with great difficulty, and made a couple of faltering steps towards the sidewalk before it overbalanced. The figure had overbalanced because it wasn't used to being without arms.

Phillippa screamed.

She scratched, and bit, and kicked, and tore her way through the people who encompassed her. As she stepped onto the paveline the hurricane helped her on her way.

Ahead of her the figure again raised itself to its knees. It managed to get one foot beneath its weight, but as soon as it tried to rise it toppled sideways once more.

'Nick! Nick!' she shrieked, as she ran along the moving paveline, but her words were lost in the wind.

Phillippa was caught and overtaken by a whirlwind of refuse which the air blast had collected from the Blue Star Club. There were bouncing stahlex cans, discarded bags of angel biscuits, and empty felicity packets, which bowled along with all the other rubbish that had been swept out of the sidewalks.

The suction from the vacuum pump became increasingly powerful as the paveline approached the terminus. Nick turned slowly over, rocked, and rolled back. Then he turned over again, and then again, and soon he was turning like a piece of wood which rolls down the beach in the wake of an ebbing wave.

Phillippa tried to scream again, but no sound came.

Nick didn't stop rolling until she reached the spot and flung herself on top of him. She put her arms around him and he did not resist.

'I love you, Nick, I love you,' she sobbed, as she covered his face with kisses.

Nick Levantine opened his mouth to say something, and he was still trying to tell Phillippa what he thought about her when, locked together, they were swallowed by the much bigger mouth of the vacuum pump.

During the first minutes of its operation the scavenger system had fulfilled the office of a benevolent ocean current, sweeping a living soup into the mouth of a feeding whale. It was as if a limitless supply of plankton had been photosynthesized under the artificial sun of the thruway.

The glut had quickly disappeared, however. An

occasional morsel was separated from its finger holds on the smooth façades of the beeblocks, where people hung like limpets. But the swarming life of the compound was draining away through the Gatehouse, and the rest who were still wriggling to get through were no longer within the range of suction. The real feast was over.

In any case, the vacuum pump was suffering from a surfeit, and the pains of indigestion manifested themselves in a succession of grinding hiccups and retching groans, which gradually became transformed into the sound of rotors slithering to a halt. With a fullthroated cough the vacuum pump gobbed a half-digested stew onto the paveline, and the moving paveline promptly washed it back into the seething gullet which then spewed it out again.

The paveline continued to play the part of determined nurse, while the vacuum pump bubbled and dribbled like an overfed baby.

44

THE WALLS OF THE TINY MODULE were faced with mirrors to give an illusion of space.

She tilted back her head and closed her eyes, and when he kissed her small, freckled nose, and throat, and eyelids, it seemed to him that each kiss was multiplied by itself until he showered an illimitable number of kisses upon her upturned face. The sides of this little room expanded to accommodate the boundless immensity of his love, reflecting it across infinity, like a variation on the same theme repeated for ever, until the refracted image filled every corner of the universe.

Meriol slowly withdrew her face. 'Is there anything else you want me to explain?'

'I don't think so.' He hesitated. 'But how did you know I would come to the Fiesta Club in the first place?'

'I didn't. An aphrodolly had been selected who suited your gestalt requirements, just as in the case of the other two. I wasn't instructed to take over from her until your reaction to me had been observed.' She lowered her eyes.

'What did the aphrodolly selected for me look like?'

She raised her eyes and smiled. 'Rather like me. I'm glad you never saw her.'

'It wouldn't have made any difference.'

Meriol freed herself from his arms, and opened a mirrored door. As Jan followed her along a narrow passageway he pondered on everything she'd told him. It had taken him long enough to discover that she was one of the rebels, he thought wryly, but she'd recognized him as an Executive as soon as he'd begun pretending to drink his beer.

At the end of the passageway she slid open a shutter. Jan smelt the salt air and looked out. The moon was rolling smoothly like a big, sand-blasted bearing in the well-greased ball-race of its orbit around the night sky. He looked to the right. The Viking waves of the North Sea, speckled with flakes of light like metallic shreds from a craftsman's bench, unfolded their lengths onto the pale sand.

'The world outside,' she murmured over his shoulder. 'A real sky, and real trees. And the sea.'

Jan looked to the left. The fractionating tower pointed its silver finger at the stars, and the red eye of Taurus stared unwinking through the cold air above the Metals Plant.

A twenty-four hour collapse in the order-intake had been sufficient. The increasing coldness of the city testified that the plant and all its systems were on total stop.

Meriol sensed his thoughts. 'Bendix was the only Executive who was on our side by conviction,' she said.

He nodded, admitting that he'd missed all the clues. The Wallenstein complex, the passion for the old Northumbria, his superior ability, and his freedom to move in the Executive world, must have all combined to make Bendix the natural leader of the rebels.

'How did you cut the window?' he asked.

'It's only steel,' she said. 'We discovered that the wall around the monorail is only made from steel plates.'

Jan leaned his elbows on the window sill and looked down. Beneath him the southbound arm of the monorail disappeared into the wall.

At regular intervals a suspended car appeared beneath the monorail, and hummed into the opening below the window. All the cars were empty now, but they were travelling at speeds which would have killed anyone who attempted to jump into one of them.

'What will they do when they find out you betrayed them?'

She shrugged. 'The same as they will do to you.'

Jan thought of what had happened to Nick and to Val Steinberg, and of what would happen to the other Executives when they were hunted down. He couldn't help any of them now. With a violent effort he directed his thoughts towards the present problem.

'Will you do what I want?' he asked.

'Yes. Anything.'

Jan led the way back along the secret passage way. On left and right were the doors of rebel modules, but the inmates were all away, marching with the revolutionaries.

In the module Meriol raised her arms to his shoulders, and looked into his face with wide eyes. Then she clung to him desperately, as if she were adrift in a wide, unfamiliar sea.

Jan looked round the interior of the module.

With the chairs folded away, and the cupboards concealed behind their mirrored doors, the room was featureless except for one of the stahlex figures which served the rebel forces as a shibboleth.

It was Paul Steinberg who had made the figures. Jan thought of the agony with which he must have worked, trying desperately to create something which would have meaning in a world which had ceased to understand. And added to the pain of the artist there was the pain of being rejected by the outside world. The outside world where men were free.

Jan knelt beside the stahlex figure, and with his eyes traced the narrow strip along its course until he found one of the ends, which terminated in the finger of a hand. When he pulled, the obedient material began to unravel like a ball of wool. The fingers disappeared, followed by the hand, then the forearm, then the rest of the arm including the shoulder.

Jan threaded the freed end through the inside handle of the main door, pulled until he had about a metre to play with, and secured it firmly with a repeated series of knots. As he carried the one-armed figure into the passageway, the head unwound and spiralled behind him.

At the window he set the mutilated figure down, knelt, and found the remaining end in a finger of the other hand. He pulled free a long length of the stahlex strip, judged it with his eyes, and withdrew some more. With nimble fingers he made a loop, and clinched the noose with another series of knots.

'Are you ready?' he asked, smiling.

Meriol nodded.

He moved to the window, and leaned out. The
first attempt was a failure. When the second car
approached, however, he judged the distance
more accurately and dropped the swinging loop of
stahlex strip over the leading wheels of the bogie.

'Stand back!' he ordered.

With an abrupt *pingg* the figure unwound from
neck to hip and from hip to toe. In the blink of an
eye all those hours of loving labour were quite
undone. The stahlex strip sang and shimmered in
the passageway, tighter than a bow string, as the
linear motor of the monorail car put it under ten-
sion.

Jan pushed his shoulders into the window and
wriggled forwards. The back of the monorail car
was almost beneath him. He dropped heavily, but
scrambled to his feet as quickly as he could. The
following car was certain to burst the knots he had
tied.

'Drop!' he yelled.

Meriol's head and shoulders appeared, as she
pushed herself forward. The car was shuddering
throughout its length, and the linear motor whined
on a more querulous note as it strove to drive the
vehicle a few more centimetres into the tunnel. On
a lower key Jan heard the humming of the next car.

'Drop!' he shouted again.

There was a loud bang as the defective stahlex
burst open along the interface. Jan was thrown
backwards, so that he involuntarily compensated
for the forward movement of the car and broke her
fall.

They rushed forward into the darkness, and the
noise of the monorail echoed around them like sea
waves in an underground cavern. Jan folded her in
his arms, to await the appearance of a new sky.

45

THE REBEL HORDE marched down the long, straight road with trees on each side.

The experience in the autopark had been frustrating. They'd discovered that there was little they could do to damage the panoramic windows and shell-formed bodies. So they'd had to content themselves with turning the three autos over onto their curved roofs, and leaving them rocking on their backs like turtles.

After that, several gangs continued along the coast road towards the Executive homes.

The main force, however, swung off towards the works. For them it was the Valhalla of hated gods, and when they saw the ornamental stahlex gate they felt that they were approaching the very citadel of tyranny.

The gate opened at the approach of the leaders, and the rebels entered an avenue overshadowed by the branches of trees.

Then they halted.

At the other end of the avenue a figure had appeared, and it walked towards them with confident strides. But as the figure approached they saw that the face was creased in a welcoming smile, and amiable wrinkles ran from the corners of the photocells which served as eyes.

'Welcome to the British works of the Stahlex Corporation,' called Henry.

With a loud whoop, and yells of laughter, the mob broke into a forward run. Henry advanced towards them, his smile never faltering, and his step never failing, until he was swept off his feet.

They found that Henry was even more difficult to mutilate than the autos had been. Three centuries of experience in making nuts and bolts, and in manipulating metals, had preceded the manufacture of the GK Series 7B. And whereas the autos, overturned and supine, had given the rebels some sense of victory, Henry was different because he kept moving about.

'The trees which overhang our path are cedars of Lebanon,' Henry told them. 'You will notice that the branches, at first ascending, become horizontal . . .'

The leaders left him to his own devices, and proceeded onwards to the works. Henry chatted away on his back, pointing with an unjointed index finger, and pausing for questions which never came.

A following group of rebels interrupted their advance and tried to restrain the moving legs. All their efforts were without success, until the legs came together of their own accord and ceased their operations.

'Those extremely tall trees are Douglas Firs,' said Henry pointing vaguely out to sea. 'They rise to a height of over 70 metres, and we are particularly proud of them.'

The legs started to move again.

There are a lot more
where this one came from!

ORDER your FREE catalog of ACE paperbacks here. We have hundreds of inexpensive
books where this one came from priced from
75¢ to $2.50. Now you can read all the books
you have always wanted to at tremendous
savings. Order your *free* catalog of ACE
paperbacks now.

ACE BOOKS ● Box 576, Times Square Station ● New York, N.Y. 10036